Charles T. Brooks

The Jobsiad

SALZWASSER
VERLAG

Charles T. Brooks

The Jobsiad

Reprint of the original, first published in 1863.

1st Edition 2022 | ISBN: 978-3-37500-223-7

Verlag (Publisher): Salzwasser Verlag GmbH, Zeilweg 44, 60439 Frankfurt, Deutschland
Vertretungsberechtigt (Authorized to represent): E. Roepke, Zeilweg 44, 60439 Frankfurt, Deutschland
Druck (Print): Books on Demand GmbH, In de Tarpen 42, 22848 Norderstedt, Deutschland

The Jobsiad

A

GROTESCO-COMICO-HEROIC POEM

FROM THE GERMAN

OF

Dr. Carl Arnold Kortum

BY

CHARLES T. BROOKS

PHILADELPHIA:

1863.

TRANSLATOR'S PREFACE.

Carl Arnold Kortüm, the author of this unique poem—which may almost be said to form a genus by itself—was born at Mühlheim in 1745, and died as Physician, at Bochum, a small town in Westphalia, in 1824, in the eightieth year of his age. If we knew the particulars of his life, we might perhaps find in him an answer to Solomon's question in regard to laughter: "What doeth it?" namely, It prolongeth man's days.

The *Jobsiad* enjoys a great and general popularity in its native country,* and is, of course, a particular

---

* In Marggraff's *House-treasury of German humor* occurs the following:—

"The *Jobsiad* first appeared anonymously in 1784, and has now reached its Tenth Edition, [of several thousand copies each] which may well be regarded as a proof of the power of this jolly book to stand the test of time. A book *may* attain to several editions in swift succession, and then after all be suddenly forgotten or no more read; but when, after half a century, new editions of a book are still called

favorite of students, several of whom the translator has heard recite passages from it—"pompously squaring the circle described by the wrinkle round the mouth," as Jean Paul says of Schoppe—with exceeding richness of comic effect. Perhaps, indeed, to be perfectly

---

for and pass out of print again,—this is certainly a proof of its having a kernel of national and lasting vitality. The *Jobsiad* owes the popularity which it still continues to find as well to its drastic drollery in the invention and management of characters and situations, and their ethico-historical interest, as to the circumstance, that pedantry, with its innumerable absurdities, (which, indeed, forms the main object of this comic poem) has not even to this day died out in Germany, and will hardly ever die out, though it should from time to time assume different forms. The treatment betrays an original *vis comica* and a naive drollery such as are at this day seldom found; nay, the comic rises sometimes even to humor, insofar as we may regard it as one of the peculiarities of humor, that the Poet tosses about the world, which he sees at his feet, with sovereign caprice, with an ideal whimsicality, that never suffers itself to be degraded, by the follies on which it exercises its persiflage, to the level of hypochondriacal moodiness or a schoolmaster-like pedantry. . . . . . . The *Jobsiad* owes a great part of its effect to the peculiar doggerel, since become typical, managed by him with the most riotous extravagance of whimsy, and yet at the same time with the sure hand of a master, which Kortüm, with happy hit, himself originally created for his epic."

enjoyed and appreciated, ſuch a production ſhould be heard as read by ſome one who has the ſkill and ſpirit to give it the proper tone and *twang*, or, perhaps, it might advantageouſly be accompanied with a ſcale of muſical and *naſal* intonation.

By way of giving the reader all the help the caſe ſeems to admit, in the abſence of the deſiderata juſt referred to, the tranſlator will add a few remarks in reſpect to rhyme and rhythm.

It will be obſerved, as one of the commoneſt requirements in making out the meaſure and ſecuring the comic effect, that all ſorts of liberties are taken, for inſtance, with accent. Thus, for the ſake of rhyme, ſuch words as *Baron*, *Turkey*, *Father*, and many others, have the ſtreſs transferred to the laſt ſyllable; and ſo, too, *frequently*, *contrary*, *neceſſary*, will ſometimes have the emphaſis thrown on the laſt ſyllable but one.—Equal licence is allowed in ſpelling. *Swabia* is ſpelt *Swaby* to rhyme with *baby*. *Nature* is ſpelt *Natur* to rhyme with *Senater*. The final *g* is repeatedly cut off from participles. Thus *ſpinning* becomes *ſpinnin'* for the ſake of making it rhyme with *women*. —But the reader's Yankee ſenſe will do juſtice to all theſe things as he goes along, and practice will beget ſmoothneſs, the rough quality being gradually worn off by the friction and heat of a rapid movement.

One word more in regard to the metre of this rampant doggerel, and the translator, with the author, commits his work to the "indulgent reader." The metre is certainly somewhat *particular metre.* The shortest and most satisfactory key to be given for the scanning is to say, boldly, that each line consists of four feet, each foot containing as many or few syllables as the case may require. We will give a specimen, trusting that the reader will then feel competent to career with great rapidity, precision and satisfaction over the roughnesses that most seriously

"Shake the rackt axle of Art's rattling car,"

and the occasional extended tracts of verse, that might otherwise prove to some readers in this fast age a *dead man's journey.*

Take, then, the following, which we divide, thus :—(the odd syllable over and above the four feet in the first couplet being a mere flourish, or *kick-up* of the last foot—the hind foot, so to speak, of the *quadruped*) :—

"If ōne | of his pā | tients chānced | to recōv | er,
| It was trūm | petēd | the coūn | try ō | ver,
And they sāid | behōld! | the fā | mous mān |
Has wroūght | a wōn | drous cūre | agāin.!

"But if he happened to lose his patients,
Or they died in the midst of his operations,
'Twas then: He died for want of breath,
There's not an herb growing 's a cure for death."

The *Jobsiad* will already have had a certain introduction and commendation in this country by the four genial pictures of Hasenclever, now in Philadelphia, the first representing Jobs as he comes home to his astonished family from the University, the second as he appears before the Clerical Board of Examiners as a candidate for the ministry, the third, as a schoolmaster, and the fourth, as night-watchman. These pictures were for a long time on exhibition at the Düsseldorf Gallery in New York, and the two chapters of this translation containing Jobs's letter to his parents for money, when he was at college, and the elder Jobs's answer, were printed in full in the catalogue of the exhibition, having originally appeared, (the first and only portion of the *Jobsiad* ever printed till then in English) in the "Literary World," at that time under the tasteful, spirited and generous management of the brothers Duyckinck, whose kindness the translator here gratefully remembers.

CONTENTS.

CHAPTER I.

CHAPTER II.

CHAPTER III.

CHAPTER IV.

CHAPTER V.

B

CHAPTER VI.

CHAPTER VII.

CHAPTER VIII.

CHAPTER IX.

CHAPTER X.

CHAPTER XI.

CHAPTER XII.

CHAPTER XX.

CHAPTER XXI.

CHAPTER XXII.

CHAPTER XXIII.

CHAPTER XXIV.

CHAPTER XXV.

CHAPTER XXVI.

CHAPTER XXVII.

CHAPTER XXVIII.

CHAPTER XXIX.

CHAPTER XXX.

CHAPTER XXXI.

CHAPTER XXXII.

CHAPTER I.

Preface, and the Author sets out to describe the story of Hieronimus Jobs, deceased, and he gives his little book the paternal benediction.

RESPECTED READER! for thy edification,
And likewise for my own recreation,
A superfine history I plan,
Of Hieronimus Jobs, a remarkable man.

2. Of whom I have many things to mention,
Deserving your particular attention,
And who, in all this life's queer muss,
Was a curious Hieronimus.

3. To tell all about him were out of the question,
'Twould be too much for the reader's digestion,
And paper and space would be quite too small
To recite his adventures each and all.

4. I have respecting him many Data,
But confine myself to the prominent Fata,
And tell what he did from the day of his birth
That was most memorable on the earth.

5. Now, as I have received from St. Apollo
The laudable gift of rhyme, it will follow
That instead of telling my tale in prose
A very fine kind of verse I chose.

6. I may not always adopt that measure
In which a cultivated ear finds pleasure;
The indulgent reader will consider meanwhile
That this is what they call the *popular style*.

7. From my ancestor, old Hans Sachs, I inherit
As a second nature, the rhyming merit,
Hence it is that I hold poesy so dear,
And relate all things in verses here.

8. There's nobody but that rehearses
My cousin, the Wandsbeck messenger's verses,
And yet, compared with my fabric, you'll find
That his are very far behind.

9. I have at the ſame time labored buſily,
As the indulgent reader will ſee very eaſily,
To have the book, as was right and good,
Adorned with fine engravings in wood.

10. But as new engravings were ſcarce and coſtly,
I have borrowed from other ſources moſtly,
And yet it would puzzle any one to tell
That they *were* borrowed, they fit ſo well.

11. They're none of Chodowiecki's chefs-d'œuvre,
I almoſt flatter myſelf, however,
They will do as well, or well enough,
To help the book through a world ſo rough.

12. And, then, if the pictures are not the neateſt,
The verſes, too, are not the completeſt,
And ſo the two exactly agree
And make out a perfect harmony.

13. And now little Book, I'll no longer delay thee;
Go hence, to the ſons of men diſplay thee;
There's many a book no better than thou,
Is yearly ſent to the Fair, I trow.

14. And yet allow me one moment to linger,
While I place on thy head my authorial finger,
And like a father benignantly,
Pronounce, dear Book, a bleſſing on thee!

15. May heaven protect thee a good long ſeaſon
From critics, moths and lamp-paper treaſon,
And all other miſchiefs that await
Printed books at the preſent date.

16. Thou wilt have, both in and out of Swaby,
Thy native land, many readers, may be;
That paper, printing and labor of brain,
May not, God help us! have been in vain.

17. Go now and with my greetings hie thee
To all and each who read and buy thee,
And to every worſhipful Reviewer,
My ſpecial compliments, be ſure.

18. Tell them,(but ſoftly, that they may not be offended,)
How they have often reviewed and recommended,
Many a book before now,
That was much worſe written than thou.

Notes.

Stanza 8. The *Wandſbeck meſſenger* means that ſimple-hearted old German, Claudius, born in 1743, who so called himself and took for the motto of his papers, "*Aſmus, omnia ſua ſecum portans.*" (Aſmus, carrying all his poſſeſſions with him.)

Stanza 10. And yet the *learned* reader will detect in the wood cut that heads this chapter, the traditionary picture of St. Luke, attended by the Ox, and writing his goſpel.

Stanza 11. Chodowiecki was a famous German artiſt in this line, born at Dantzic in 1723.

CHAPTER II.

Of the parents of our hero and how he was born, and of a memorable dream which his mother had.

BEFORE I go further, it is my intention,
Of our hero's two parents to make mention,
And a word or two muſt be alſo ſet forth
Concerning his true place of birth.

2. It was, then, a little town in Swaby,
Where the parents lived who had this baby,
And there his father, Hans Jobs by name,
Was a counſellor of conſiderable fame.

3. He was rich in cattle and that ſort of bleſſing,
Beſide our hero many other children poſſeſſing,
Of the male ſex and female no leſs,
And lived, on the whole, in peace and happineſs.

4. He had in wine ſome little dealings,
Was an upright man in his walk and feelings,
Juſt both at home and in council hall,
And a great economiſt withal.

5. A genuine Lutheran in his religious perſuaſion,
In philoſophy neither Wolfian nor Carteſian,
Becauſe in fact neither Wolf nor Kant
Noı any philoſophy could he underſtand.

6. To ſtudy, however, he had ſomewhat attended,
And for a whole year the gymnaſium frequented,
And conſequently, ſo far, knew much more
Than any worſhipful counſellor had done before.

7. When poor folks came, he loved to befriend them,
And for a pledge would gladly lend them,
And never charged more than ten per cent,
And was ſomewhat phlegmatic in temperament.

8. He was rather ſhort and ſquat in ſtature,
Was endowed with a great appetite by nature,
The newspapers he loved to read,
And ſmoked many a pipe of narcotic weed.

9. And often when the gall ran over,
Severe attacks of gout he would ſuffer,
And yet he always found himſelf able
To take his place at the council table.

10. The mother was of reſpectable ſtation,
The moſt eloquent woman in the Swabian nation,
Tall and virtuous and upright,
And meek as a lamb—*at firſt ſight.*

11. Only, alas! as too often the caſe is
Not only here, but in other places,
She now and then, when it came in her way,
Would wear the breeches, as they ſay.

12. Now this occaſioned no ſmall vexation
At times, and led to altercation;
Yet on the whole did our two loves
Live like a pair of turtle doves.

13. They had now for ſeveral years in ſucceſſion
Received of children a yearly addition,
And yet at the time of our ſtory, 'twas plain
Mrs. Jobs was ſoon to come down again.

14. And now, when her nine months were ended,
And the time of delivery impended;
The above Mrs. Jobs immediately went
To make preparation for the important event.

15. Before, however, I go on with my hiſtory,
I muſt ſtop to mention a ſingular myſtery,
A dream, in fact, that one night befel
This Mrs. Jobs of whom I tell.

16. We learn by experience oft repeated,
That dreams are not to be lightly treated;
Of that, dear reader, I presently
A notable proof will furnish thee.

17. One night, as Mrs. Jobs lay sleeping,
This wonderful dream into her head came creeping,
That, instead of a little child, was born
Of her a great and mighty horn.

18. This horn so mightily crashed and sounded,
That Mrs. Jobs woke up astounded,
And often, after she awoke,
About that horn she thought and spoke.

19. A lady, to whom she applied for explanation,
Gave her at the time this consolation,
That thus the interpretation ran:
Her child would certainly be a great man.

20. And that his voice his mouth would nourish,
And in the pulpit would greatly flourish,
For that was clearly and finely shown
By the monstrous horn with its mighty tone.

21. But we will not here be anticipating
The sequel for which the reader is waiting,
And so I now return to the text
And proceed to tell what happened next.

22. The mother laid all things straight in her chamber,
And on the thirtieth day of September,
Just at the right time she had the joy
Of giving birth to a little boy.

23. Was ever a father's happineſs greater?
And heavens! how proudly felt the Senátor!
And how did he leap, when, blooming there,
He saw before him a son and heir!

Notes.

Stanza 2. *Swaby*, poetic licence for Swabia, juſt as we have *Virginny* for Virginia, and for Arabia, *Araby* (the Bleſt.)

Stanza 7. Some points in this description of old Jobs will remind the reader of "Old Grimes."

CHAPTER III.

How Mrs. Jobs, in child-bed, received a visit from her female friends, and what Ma'am Gossip Schnepperle prophecied of the child.

AND so Mrs. Jobs, as we've juſt been telling,
With her dear little Jobſey was keeping her dwelling;
Cloſe by her ſide all ſwaddled he lay,
And thought of nothing and ſlept away.

2. 'Twere impoſſible to deſcribe the jubilation
That filled all the Jobſian habitation;
Neighbors and kinſmen came and went,
And thoſe that couldn't themſelves go, ſent.

3. The chamber rang with a conſtant alarum,
As when the bees in the May month ſwarm,
And all the day long it was buzz, buzz, buzz,
Round the dear little Hieronimus.

4. Exactly three days had now expired,
Since Mrs. Jobs to her bed retired,
When a mighty ſwarm of women made free
To invite themſelves to afternoon tea.

5. And of all theſe madams, to my thinking,
Who came to Mrs. Jobs's tea-drinking,
Though there was none whoſe gifts were ſmall,
Ma'am Schnepperle's gift excelled them all.

6. Little Jobſey's father was her couſin;
The company talked of the weather, and a dozen
Other matters of the ſame kind,
And the converſation was quite unconfin'd.

7. Next after madam's health they inquired,
And to know how the baby was they deſired,
Whether he ſeemed to like his pap,
And was a quiet little chap?

8. Then they began, in rotation, to raiſe him
High in the air and *beſt* him and praiſe him,
And none could find fit words to expreſs
Their ſenſe of his uncommon prettineſs.

9. "My honored coufin," began Ma'am Schnepperle,
(She fpoke through her nofe, but rather dapperly,)
A learned man the child will be,
That by his face I can plainly fee.

10. "I have read a book and admired it greatly,
Which I took from the council library lately,
About the art of Phyfiognomy,
And everything, the how and why.

11. "And there was a dreadful lot of faces,
Pious rogues with terrible grimaces,
Learn'd dunces, profiles ugly and fair,
And heads of animals, too were there.

12. "If I rightly remember what I read there,
I think (almoft in fo many words) it faid there,
That there is genius in fuch a phiz,
As this little wry one of Jobfey's is.

13. "Nor fhould I fear to pledge his mother
That the child will take to books one day or other;
And, if he only lives long enough, he
Will be a parfon, undoubtedly.

14. "His mighty voice that he lifts like a trumpet
Shows that he one day will mount the pulpit."
(N. B.—Juft here little Jobfey cried out
As if he knew what they were talking about.)

15. Ma'am faid much more before fhe had completed,
That cannot in this place be repeated;
However fhe ended at laft, and then
All the women fell in with a loud Amen.

16. And now when the visit was finally ended,
Each one her hand to Mrs. Jobs extended,
And thanked her for the honour she had done,
Then all returned to whene they'd come.

17. Poor Mrs. Jobs's head-aches were shocking,
But she was edified by Ma'am Schnepperle's talking;
Especially as the world said, she
Was acquainted with astrology.

Notes.

Stanza 3. *Swarm* in the second line must be pronounced with the Irish *r*: *swarrm.*

Stanza 8. To *heft*, was a vulgarism in New England, in the translator's boyhood, meaning to test the heaviness (*heft*) of a thing by lifting it.

Stanza 10. The book would appear to have been Lavater.

Stanza 14. *Trumpet* and *pulpit* make a fine *assonanza.*

Stanza 16. The reader will please remember the rule for scanning given in the preface.

CHAPTER IV.

How the child was baptized, and how he was named Hieronimus.

WHEN a few days more had alſo tranſpired,
'Twas baptiſm plainly the infant deſired,
For his cries were piteous to hear,
And cauſed his mother pain ſevere.

2. Vainly they plied both breaſt and bottle,
Nor would ſugar dollies ſtop his throttle,
But he kept up one inceſſant ſhriek
'Till one could no longer hear himſelf ſpeak.

3. Therefore in Senator Jobs's habitation,
Proviſion was made for the baptiſmal collation,
And diſhes of all ſorts were made or ſent
That might adorn the ſacrament.

4. Twiſts and rings and other ſuch matters,
Were baked for the ſupper and piled on platters,
Nor was there in wine, tobacco and beer,
Certainly any deficiency here.

5. Friends and relations, aunts, uncles and couſins,
Nurſes, acquaintances, neighbors by dozens,
When the hour arrived, came pouring in,
All ſmiling and dreſſed as neat as a pin.

6. That ſexton and parſon, with formulary,
Were alſo there, you need not query,
And the whole ſenatorial body, too,
Had arrived at the houſe in ſeaſon due.

7. Many other gueſts alſo, by invitation,
Came to this great and high celebration,
And to Jobs's credit confeſſed it muſt be,
That all paſſed off with propriety.

8. However there roſe a diſputation
About the infant's appellation;
Whether Heinz it ſhould be, or Peter or Hans,
Or Joſt or Jacob or Hermann or Franz.

9. But none of theſe names, though full of attraction
Seemed to give univerſal ſatisfaction,
And matters might almoſt have paſſed
From words to ſomething worſe at laſt,

10. Had not the parſon, with wiſe diſcerning,
Given this advice, like a man of learning,
To examine the calendar, and ſee,
Affixed to the birthday what name might be.

11. The calendar, without further queſtion,
Was ſtraightway opened by the ſexton,
And there they found without any fuſs,
The name of St. Hieronimus.

12. Such a wiſe counſel to all the connection,
To parents and godfathers gave great ſatisfaction,
And ſo the vote was unanimous,
That the child ſhould be called Hieronimus.

13. And now when this weighty point was decided,
The parſon, in manner and form provided,
Pronounced and performed the Actus, and thus
The child was baptized Hieronimus.

14. All things thereafter went calm and coſy,
Parſon and ſexton waxed right roſy,
And they did nothing elſe for almoſt half
The night but eat, drink, ſmoke and laugh.

CHAPTER V.

How the little child Hieronimus occupied himself.

WHILE yet in his ſwaddling clothes, Hieronimuſſy
Paſſed his time in a manner ſufficiently fuſſy,
Slept, ate, ſucked or drank, one after another,
Or liſtened the lullaby ſung by his mother.

2. His ſleeping and eating, and ſucking and drinking,
Were much like other children's, to my thinking;
Much time in rocking him alſo was ſpent,
And yet for all that he was never content;

3. But often would ſcream whole days together,
And raiſe in the cradle a bitter pother,
As if ſome terrible grief had aſſailed him,
Though there was nothing on earth that ailed him.

4. Some wiſe people have undertaken,
With an air that implied they could not be miſtaken,
To aſſert that there muſt in theſe caſes be
(God save the mark!) ſome ſorcery.

5. And ſo the nurſe and eke the phyſician
Are called to pronounce on the child's condition,
And many a doſe of rhubarb and rum
Is given, and ſometimes laudanum.

6. He thus became almoſt a burden to his mother,
But he throve in this way as well as in any other,
And every day, as it came along,
Found him more fat and stout and ſtrong.

7. Father and mother took therefore great pleaſure
In their darling child—their precious treaſure,
And many was the hearty buſs
They gave little Hieronimus.

8. I have no further information
Of the firſt few years of Jobs's earthly probation;
And therefore it is beſt, I ſuppoſe,
To bring this chapter here to a cloſe.

NOTE.

Stanza 5. "What are you doing, mad mother! miſerable nurſe! when you pour this vile compound into the unſtained ſnow of an infant's boſom! Know you not that paregoric is opium and rum? A compoſition that Samſon could not have ſwallowed much of, unſcathed." *Sermon on Intemperance.*

CHAPTER VI.

Actions and opinions of Hieronimus in his boyiſh years, and how he went to ſchool.

OF the other early years of our hero,
I likewiſe can give no information that is thorough,
Inasmuch as the courſe his life has run,
Has been hitherto a very narrow one.

2. Conſequently an account of his actions,
Would poſſeſs no remarkable attractions;
Suffice it to ſay, that while yet a boy,
Eating and drinking were his chief employ.

3. He had however his giſts as well as others,
Preferred as playmates the girls to their brothers,
Would often quarrel and teaſe in play,
And was noted for many a miſchievous way.

4. Lying and ſwearing he early took to,
And learned them well without any book too,
Whereby the neighbours' children round
Much edification in his company found.

5. He had a ſweet tooth, loved candy to diſtraction,
Likewiſe in nuts and raisins took great ſatisfaction,
And all the money he got and ſpent,
For ſomething dainty and liquoriſh went.

6. With brothers and ſiſters he always was quarrelling,
But his father never would give him a feruling,
And as to his mother, poor, dear, good soul
She never noticed ſuch things at all.

7. All children of his age he could maſter,
There was none of them could leap or run faſter,
Not one of them was ſo ſtrong as he,
And whoever provoked him had better let him be.

8. And being a boy of great endowments,
He was charged with many houſehold employments,
To foddering the cattle would ſometimes ſee,
And ſuperintend the economy.

9. Sometimes he rode the horſes to water,

Or a jug of beer from the tavern brought, or
A fresh laid egg from the hennery,
Or a goose's or duck's, as the caſe might be.

10. On the whole, was a fair, good-for-nothing fellow,
Had a pair of lungs that could terribly bellow,
And would act on a bench the preacher's part;
All this went right to his parents' heart.

11. For they watched with a ſecret gratification
Hieronimus's talent in its manifeſtation,
And often in their heads it would run:
"There is the parſon, ſure as a gun."

12. Eſpecially the mother, who remembered
The Schnepperle's words, when she was chambered,
And alſo the dream ſhe formerly had,
Could hardly contain herſelf, ſhe was ſo glad.

13. For all ſeemed to hang together ſo neatly,
And expreſs the matter ſo completely;
And when ſhe weighed all this, ſhe could ſee
The future parſon as plain as could be.

14. Accordingly to ſchool they ſent him,
To fit him for the ſtation they meant him,
Which pleaſed Hieronimus little enough,
For he liked his play much better than ſuch ſtuff.

15. He hated his leſſons and never learned them,
He threw his books on the floor or burned them,
And the a, b, abs and the o, b, obs
They gave a head-ache to maſter Jobs.

16. 'Tis true, the preceptor did earneſtly endeavour
To recommend learning to his favour,
And he and the rod in company,
Worked away at his genius faithfully.

17. This man had remarkable qualifications
For giving ſelf-willed boys educations,
And oftentimes on ſhoulder and back
His cane came down with a mighty thwack.

18. Extraordinary efforts in this caſe were needed,
But at length the Herculean labor ſucceeded,
And Hieronimus his letters told,
By the time he was about ten years old.

19. How old he may have been exactly,
When he learned to read the German correctly,
I am not at preſent prepared to ſtate
In a manner very accurate.

20. And when more years he began to reckon,
From the German ſchòol the boy was taken,
And to the Latin ſchool was ſent
To learn his Latin; but how it went

21. With Hieronimus in his Latin,
And how they ſucceeded in getting *that* in,
All this I promiſe faithfully,
The reader ſhall in the next chapter ſee.

CHAPTER VII.

How the boy Hieronimus went to the Latin ſchool, and how he did not learn much there.

HIERONIMUS, purſuing the parental intention,
Began now at Menſa his Firſt Declenſion,
And every important article taught
In the Latin grammar he likewiſe got.

2. Many vocables he alſo committed,
But the poor Hieronimus was much to be pitied,
For that cursèd louſy Latin, he ſaid,
Would nowiſe get into his head.

3. In Conjugations and Syntaxis,
And generally in the Latin Praxis,
It ſeemed as if the old Harry was looſe,
And his body ſuffered no little abuſe.

4. For the Rector being a Hypochondriacus
Showed no partiality to Hieronimus,
But cudgelled him often as if he were mad,
And many a ſkinfull he gave the poor lad.

5. By a ſyſtem of teaching ſo painfully hurried,
The youth almoſt to death was worried,
And often wiſhed (in terms uncivil)
His grim old Rector would go to the d——l.

6. 'Tis true, full many a trick he played him,
And richly for all the cudgellings paid him,
In fact the man had a deal of fuſs
With the rogue of a Hieronimus.

7. For he cut up incognito all ſorts of capers
With the old gentleman's perukes and papers,
And ſent full many a poiſoned dart
Right into the worthy man's heart.

8. He gave his ſchoolmates, too, much trouble,
And brought them into many a hobble,
For he hated them with hatred profound,
And often knocked them flat on the ground.

9. No book of theirs, nor any garment
Was ſafe from the tricks of this torment,
And many of his tricks were of that kind,
That leave a very bad odour behind.

10. Sometimes he would act the eavesdropper,
And catching a ſchoolmate at anything improper,
Straightway he to the Rector reported the boy,
And witneſſed the flogging with heartfelt joy.

11. Lazy in brain and ſore in body,
At length he went home quite ſick of ſtudy,
And there for the moſt part his time paſſed by
In unprofitable inactivity.

12. Of his Greek I have nothing to ſay at preſent,
He found it exceedingly unpleaſant,
And the barbarous Tupto, Tupteis,
Would turn Hieronimus' heart to ice.

13. Far be it from me, thought he, to dabble
In ſuch a jaw-cracking, Iriſh gabble,
And as regards the Hebrew ſpeech,
He called it poiſon and kept out of its reach.

14. He made therefore no progreſs worth repeating,
Save in lying and ſwearing and drinking and eating,
And in the invention of an original cuss,
Nobody could match Hieronimus.

NOTE.

Stanza 14. *Cuss* is Yankee for *curse*. (*Note for foreign readers.*)

CHAPTER VIII.

How Hieronimus's parents, with the Rector and other friends, took counſel what they ſhould make out of the boy.

Now when the boy in this ſtate of diſtraction,
Had paſſed ſome eighteen years and a fraction,
And in fact was already half a head higher
Than old Hans Jobs his ſire,

2. His parents began to be puzzled with cogitation
About his future occupation,
For it was high time ſomething ſhould be done
With this moſt extraordinary ſon.

3. Firſt of all they put the Rector the queſtion,
Whether he could not make any ſuggeſtion
As to his future deſtiny,
And what he was beſt fitted to be.

4. Now this man would not diſſemble in the matter,
Nor with idle hopes the parents flatter,
So he came out roundly and told the truth:
"You can't make anything good of the youth.

5. "Study is clearly not his vocation;
It were wiſer to try ſome occupation;
A Counſellor might of ſuch a one be made;
If not, it were well to put him to a trade.

6. "I have many a time in recitation
Diſcovered with great commiſeration,
That there's nothing in him that poſſibly could
Do a reſpected public the leaſt mite of good."

7. This ſpeech, as may well be apprehended,
The Jobſian couple grievouſly offended;
They heaped upon it all manner of abuſe
And called the Rector a ſtupid gooſe.

8. In a council of friends the queſtion was ſtated,
And pro et contra rationally debated;
Old Jobs looked as grave, and ſo did all,
As if that houſe were the council hall.

9. After they had been two-and-a-half hours in ſeſſion
They compromiſed matters by this propoſition:
That the ſubject be poſtponed to a new term
For nearer examination; meanwhile we adjourn.

CHAPTER IX.

How the gipſy Urgalindina was alſo conſulted about Hieronimus, who underſtood the chiromantic art.

AND now all the friends who the meeting attended,
At Counſellor Jobs's, homeward had wended,
When, as good luck would have it, one day,
There came an old gipſy along that way.

2. From a very old family ſhe was deſcended,
Urgalindina was her name, ſhe pretended,
And Egypt, ſhe ſaid, was the country from which
She came, and her mother was burned as a witch.

3. Men's actions and fortunes this woman predicted,
When ſhe the lines on their hands had inſpected,
And future things as clearly could trace
As if they already had taken place.

4. She had greatly delighted many a maiden
By propheſying her approaching weddin',
And indicated the bridegroom's name
As if ſhe had long been acquainted with the ſame.

5. To many an heir beginning to be diſcontented,
The ſpeedy death of a rich uncle ſhe hinted,
And oh, how glad would ſuch a one be,
When his uncle died unexpectedly!

6. To many almoſt deſpairing ſpouſes,
Whoſe wives, alas! were the plagues of their houſes,
She came with welcome words of cheer
And whiſpered a ſpeedy deliverance near.

7. To many a dunce diſagreeably ſmelling
Of muſk and pomatum, ſhe was often ſeen telling
How, in ſpite of all his awkwardneſs,
He would find ſome fair one his heart to bleſs.

8. The words ſhe choſe were always ſo fitting
That ſhe hardly ever failed of hitting;
Yet a cunning ambiguity
Helped her out of many a perplexity.

9. She had for each ſome ſpecial good ſtory:
To ſoldiers ſhe propheſied powder and glory,
To deſtitute epicures heaps of gold,
The kingdom of heaven to matrons old.

10. With other arts ſhe was alſo acquainted,
But not all her ſingular merits prevented
Her falling occaſionally into ſin,
For ſhe ſtole, incidentally, now and then.

11. In short her reputation rivaled in ſplendor,
The fame of the celebrated witch of Endor,
At leaſt in lying and chiromancy
No gipſy woman was keener than ſhe.

12. Now when Mrs. Jobs heard of her coming,
She immediately went to find the woman,
And at her door, juſt out of her reach,
Addreſſed to her the following ſpeech:

13. "My dear Mrs. Urgalindina, right glad am
I to ſee you on the preſent occaſion, Madam,
I've a ſon I beg that you would ſee,
And pronounce on his future deſtiny.

14. "I truſt you will yield to our perſuaſion,
And without any equivocation or evaſion
Very candidly ſtate to us,
What is to be done with Hieronimus."

15. "Madam!" ſhe anſwered, "I will do as directed,
So ſoon as I his hands have inſpected;
I will then, as an honeſt woman, declare
His future fortune, to a hair."

16. They immediately ſent for Hieronimus,
And Ma'am Urgalindina in a ſomewhat ominous
Tone, requeſted his right hand to ſee
Which ſomewhat ſmutty happened to be.

17. The gipſy woman, with ſearching viſion,
Examined all points with great preciſion,
Meaſured the lines and the ſurfaces too,
As chiromantiſts are wont to do.

18. For a moment or two ſhe nothing uttered,
At laſt like a Delphian Sibyl ſhe muttered
Something between her teeth a while,
And propheſied in the following ſtyle:

19. "I've ſounded, my dear Hieronimus, I've ſounded,
By the art in which I am perfectly grounded,
Thy whole future deſtiny, my ſon!
By that throat of thine and its mighty tone—

20. "Shall many a brazen villain be ſhaken,
Many a ſlumbering ſinner ſhalt thou awaken,
So that the city far and wide,
Shall by thy gifts be edified.

21. "Both good and evil ſhall feel thy protection,
Thou ſhalt guard from body's and ſoul's deſtruction
Both young and old, and great and ſmall,
A faithful and vigilant keeper to all.

22. "Thy wiſe teachings this city's population
Shall one day hear with edification,
And when thy mouth is opened to cry
Aloud, no one ſhall make reply.

23. "I may not for the preſent, venture
Any farther than this on thy future to enter,
But what I have ſaid muſt now ſuffice,
Go then, my ſon, now go and be wiſe."

24. Here Urgalindina her prophecy ended,
Both father and mother, who had cloſely attended,
Were entirely ſatisfied and filled with joy,
To hear ſuch prediction concerning their boy.

25. For in their minds already our hero
Was clearly a parſon in futuro,
With this the prophecy ſeemed to agree,
How could it be clearer poſſibly?

26. Off did Urgalindina hobble,
When ſhe had got a ſumptuous fee for her trouble;
They ſay ſhe had ſcarcely got out of ſight,
When ſhe laughed at parents and ſon outright.

27\. And now, to cover the Rector with confufion,
Both Mr. and Mrs. Jobs came to the conclufion,
That the beloved Hieronimus
Should ftraightway become a Theologus.

28\. In chapter Tenth, we fhall therefore accompany
Hieronimus to the Academy;
But firft we muft ftop awhile to tell
What took place at the laft farewell.

NOTE.

Stanza 2. The reader must be careful not to pronounce *witch* and *which* as if they were the same word, as school-boys sometimes do.

CHAPTER X.

How Hieronimus took leave of his parents and brothers and ſiſters, and started for the univerſity.

WHEN Hieronimus's departure was decided,
Straightway he was ſuperfluouſly provided
With clothes, books, money and everything
That is neceſſary to ſtudying.

2. The family found ſome conſolation
In the labour and care of the preparation,
But when the parting hour drew near
On both ſides was many a bitter tear.

3. The grave old Senator Jobs's bawling,
Was juſt a regular caterwauling,
And ſobbing he gave a farewell kiſs
To his dear ſon Hieronimus.

4. And he added alſo a fatherly bleſſing,
This counſel to the youth addreſſing;
"Farewell and attend to thy ſtudies, my ſon,
That we may have joy, when all is done!

5. "If anything ſhould ever ail thee
(There may be times when money will fail thee,)
Always write without fear to me,
Whatever is wanting I'll ſend to thee!"

6. Hieronimus was, as may well be ſuſpected,
By his father's words extremely affected,
And promiſed always to let him know
Whenever his purſe ſhould be getting low.

7. Still worſe was it with the poor mother
Who did not undertake her grief to ſmother;
Pierced through by ſorrow's bitter dart,
She preſſed her dear ſon long to her heart.

8. At length ſhe ſtepped aſide a ſecond,
And to Hieronimus beckoned,
And ſlipped into the hand of her ſonny
A little bag containing ſome money.

9. This very pious motherly bleſſing
Was to Hieronimus deeply diſtreſſing,
And not without many a heavy ſob,
He thruſt the little bag in his fob.

10. Next came his brothers and ſiſters in rotation,
Whom he, amidſt piteous lamentation,
Each by the hand ſucceſſively ſhook,
And now his departure Hieronimus took.

11. The weeping and wailing of the parents laſted
For ſeveral days; the old man faſted
To ſuch an extent as utterly to refuſe
Wine, beer, tobacco and the daily news.

12. The greateſt of all was the mother's trouble,
She was almoſt inconſolâble,
But with the brothers and ſiſters, I hear,
There was very much leſs danger to fear.

N. B.—The wood-cut that heads the next Chapter, admirably fulfils the Author's promiſe in Chapter I, 10. The *double* knave of cards expreſſes in emblem Hogier's gambling and double-dealing. One of them being knave of *hearts* alludes to the *affectionate* manner by which Hieronimus was taken in, while the hanging of the head (Kopfhängerei) betrays the hypocrite; the other being the knave of diamonds, intimates how he took all the profits as well as honors. (Stanza 29.)

The Chriſtian, or rather Pagan name *Hector* in the firſt card denotes the gay and brazen rogue, while that of *Hogier* in the ſecond ſeems to refer to the *hoax*, the humbug, he played off on Hieronimus.

CHAPTER XI.

How Hieronimus came on horseback to the post-station, and how he found at the inn a distinguished gentleman, named Herr Von Hogier, who gave him wholesome lessons, and was a knave.

AND now Hieronimus has finally departed;
The old house servant who was very kind-hearted,
Rode to the next village by his side,
Where he was to get into the postwagon to ride.

2. Altho' now the departure had affected him ſadly,
Neverthelefs he looked forward gladly
To the beloved univerſity,
Where time paſſes off ſo pleaſantly.

3. Scarcely had he began to find him-
ſelf out on the highway and Schildburg behind him,
When he parents and brothers and ſiſters forgot,
And was highly delighted at the thought,

4. That now henceforth, as a free ſtudent,
He need be no longer ſo prim and prudent,
And as to the grim old Rector and his rod,
He was well rid of them, thank God!

5. It filled him with ſpecial exultation,
He was richer than a king in his own eſtimation,
When the money into his mind did come
Which he had taken with him from home.

6. He thought and he *felt* with the greateſt pleaſure,
Of the little bag, the precious treaſure,
From his highly afflicted mother received
When ſhe at parting ſo bitterly grieved.

7. And now, as all other paſtime was wanting,
He drew out the bag and fell to counting
The money, and found to his happineſs
That the little bag contained no leſs

8. Than thirty different pieces of money,
All of ſilver, thick, heavy and ſhiny,
Gilders and dollars manifold,
Moſtly of coinage rare and old.

9. His mother had ſaved them one after another,
And for future emergencies laid them together,
For not unjuſtly ſhe had the name
Of being an economical dame.

10. Then too the ſervant who attended him
By way of paſtime occaſionally handed him
Some of the victualia
His parents had provided to eat on the way.

11. Now when in this kind of occupation,
Hieronimus had ridden ſome hours in ſucceſſion,
Faint and weary he at length got down
At the tavern of the aforeſaid town.

12. Here indeed he found the poſtwagon
In which to the univerſity he was to jog on;
But it ſo happened that the cart
Was not at the moment ready to ſtart.

13. Hieronimus firſt of all directed,
That his nag to the ſtable ſhould be conducted;
The ſervant put ſome oats in the rack,
And took the portmanteau off his back.

14. At the ſame time he began to be thinking,
Of refreſhing himſelf by eating and drinking,
And ſoon to the table he found his way,
And there grew ſtrong and freſh and gay.

15. Now there was in the tavern a fellow lodger,
With a great peruke, and a rich-looking codger,
The man from diſtant countries came,
Herr Baron von Hogier was his name.

16. The ſtranger ſhowed our hero much honour,
And inquired who he was in a friendly manner;
Hieronimus anſwered without demur,
"I am a ſtudent, reſpected ſir,

17. "At your honour's ſervice, and right glad am I
That I am going to the academy,
There to ſtudy diligently
The ſcience of theology."

18. "Ah! well, I wiſh you all the joy I can, ſir!"
The gentleman in the great peruke made anſwer,
"But, I adviſe you, take great care
That you do not get into trouble there.

19. "I in my time have had ſome knowledge
Of the way they carry on at college;
Many a young freſhman throws away
His time and money on curſéd play.

20. "And many, inſtead of ſtudying with application,
Run into all manner of diſſipation,
And waſte their valuable time
In many a folly, not to ſay crime.

21. "My own experience can anſwer
For this ſad truth, indeed it can, ſir:
I beg you therefore to attend
To what I ſay, on the word of a friend."

22. "Dear ſir," Hieronimus reſponded,
"I thank you for advice ſo candid,
And the timely wiſdom you have taught
Shall never in all my life be forgot.

23. "At the ſame time I will not diſguiſe the truth, ſir,
Playing has great attractions for this youth, ſir,
But I have the honor to aſſure you that I,
Whenever I do play, never play high."

24. "In moderate playing I ſee no danger,"
Politely anſwered the diſtinguiſhed ſtranger,
"One loſes nothing, except ennui,
And paſſes the time quite pleaſantly.

25. "We, for example, here together,
For the ſake of amuſing one another,
Might play a little game," ſaid he,
"With innocence and propriety."

26. Hieronimus, without the leaſt ſuſpicion,
Accepted the gentleman's propoſition,
And was very willing to take a game
Or two, until the poſtwagon came.

27. The thing was done as ſoon as decided,
The hoſt a new pack of cards provided
And placed before his gueſts, and ſtraightway
The two ſat down and began to play.

28. They ſet their ſtakes quite low in the beginning,
But Hieronimus, led on by his love of winning,
To mark up higher and higher begun,
Becauſe at firſt he regularly won.

29. But all on a ſudden fortune deſerted
Our hero, with whom ſhe had previouſly flirted,
And the gentleman in the great peruke
Both all the honors and profits took.

30. And thus Hieronimus had very ſoon parted
With all the looſe money he took when he ſtarted,
And now as his loſſes came thick and faſt,
He drew out the little bag at laſt.

31. And now Hieronimus began to grow frightened,
For at every throw the bag was lightened,
And it became very evident that luck
Would ſmile on the gentleman in the great peruke.

32. In leſs than three-quarters of an hour the bleſſing
Of his poor dear mother was entirely miſſing,
For the gentleman in the great peruke
Had robbed him of all by hook and crook.

33. For the good Hieronimus had not detected,
In fact he never for a moment ſuſpected,
That he was cheated by him of the great peruke,
For Herr von Hogier had an honeſt look.

34. At laſt he really began to
Think of unbuckling his portmanteau,
To ſtake the little therein contained,
Which would his reſources have entirely drained,

35. But at that moment ſo highly ominous,
The gentleman in the peruke and Hieronimus,
Both heard on a ſudden the poſtillion blow,
As a ſignal for Hieronimus to go.

36. He felt a little reluctance at parting,
Then ſuddenly and impetuouſly ſtarting,
He jumped up into the poſt-wagon and took
Leave of the gentleman in the great peruke.

CHAPTER XII.

How Hieronimus took the Poſt-wagon, and how he found therein a fair one with whom he fell in love, and who ſtole his watch.

I WILL now proceed with a narration
Of what befel Hieronimus on leaving the ſtation,
For he is not rid of his troubles yet,
But further obstacles are to be met.

2. The great peruke would ſtill come gliding
Into his thoughts as he went on riding,
And he now for the firſt time began to ſee
That the fellow no better than a knave could be.

3. His conſcience kept up a terrible racket
About the loſs of the maternal packet,
He ſighed and groaned and wiſhed bad luck
To the gentleman in the great peruke.

4. He murmured ſo that people could hear him;
But a beautiful damſel ſitting near him,
On whom his eyes till now ſcarce fell,
Rouſed him from the melancholy ſpell.

5. She ſeemed about twenty years—not older,
Black eyes and hair and a very white ſhoulder,
Roſy-red in mouth and cheek
And, the truth in a ſingle word to ſpeak,

6. Her being was nothing but grace, appealing
Irreſiſtibly to the tendereſt feeling.
This fairy inquired, half in jeſt,
What ſorrow diſturbed Hieronimus' breaſt.

7. Wherewith ſhe pleaſantly ſmiled upon him,
Which pleaſant ſmile of her's quite won him.
So that, as cloſe by her ſide he ſot,
The loſs of his packet he quite forgot.

8. A glow of rapture kindled his fancies,
For in her whole perſon and tender glances,
A youth like him could not fail to find
Something quite dangerous to his peace of mind.

9. After leſs than half an hour's duration
He had made, in beſt ſtyle, a declaration
As fervent as ever a hero of romance
Can make to his love by his author's hands.

10. She ſeemed to hear him with ſome predilection,
At all events ſhe made no objection,
Hieronimus therefore edged up more near
And began to whiſper in her ear.

11. I know not what further paſſed on the occaſion
Improper to mention in this narration,
Suffice it, with both, the time paſſed by
In ſweet, confidential familiarity.

12. When at laſt they came to the poſt-ſtation
She bade adieu with friendly proteſtation,
But in what direction ſhe went from here
Shall by and by be made to appear.

13. When, after ſeveral hours had tranſpired
Since the fair one from the carriage retired,
Hieronimus for his watch looked round,
That too had retired and was not to be found.

14. This ſecond trick of fatal termination
Was to Hieronimus a great aggravation,
For he came to the concluſion that she who left
So ſuddenly muſt have committed the theft.

15. Meanwhile nothing was left the good ſtudent
But to exerciſe patience and be more prudent,
In ſhort he determined, come what might,
To practise in future more foreſight.

16. He therefore formed a firm determination,
So ſoon as he ſhould come to the place of education,
A letter to his parents to ſend,
For a new watch and ſome money to ſpend.

17. At laſt without further moleſtation
He arrived at the place of his deſtination,
Behold therefore our Hieronimus
Henceforward an Academicus.

Note.

Stanza 3. *Luck* muſt be pronounced in a certain provincial Engliſh ſtyle, to rhyme with *peruke*.

CHAPTER XIII.

How Hieronimus at the Univerſity did diligently ſtudy Theology.

HIERONIMUS on his arrival, without heſitation,
Received, ſtante pede, his matriculation,
And ſo became immediately
A ſtudioſus of theology.

2. At univerſities, from all points of the compaſs,
Some to get knowledge and ſome to raiſe a rumpus,
Great numbers of ſtudents together are flung,
Large and little and old and young.

3. And ſo at this one from every nation
Were many in ſearch of an education,
And many new ones came every year
To proſecute various ſtudies here.

4. *Exempli gratiâ*, law and theology,
Philoſophy, medicine and coſmology,
And whatſoever other fine arts
Are needed to help them act well their parts.

5. But moſt of them, inſtead of pondering
Their ſtudies, ſet themſelves to ſquandering
Their money, fared ſumptuouſly every day
And threw their precious time away.

6 Hieronimus who liked ſtudy no better than others,
Soon joined himſelf to the merry brothers,
And very ſhortly made it appear
As if he had long been familiar here.

7. For he daily lived in *Floribus*
As well as the beſt academicus,
And many a precious night he ſpent
In carrouſing and bouſing to his heart's content.

8. Wine, beer and tobacco were his inſpiration,
And they gave his voice a fine inflation,
When he with loud and mighty clang
The *gaudeamus igitur* ſang.

9. His fellows all who gathered round him
The model of a faithful ſtudent found him,
He lived as a *burſch* of high renown
And great was his fame through all the town.

10. As to thoſe three deteſted creatures,
Philiſtines and Beadles and night-rogue-catchers,
Hieronimus as a hero true
Had often cudgelled them black and blue.

11. Many a *Pereat* he againſt them had vented,
And with ludicrous tricks their peace tormented,
And in theſe and various other ways
As a *renownist* acquired great praiſe.

12. The ſummer he ſpent in racing and riding,
And in winter was continually ſleighing and ſliding,
In ſhort Hieronimus felt himſelf free
To indulge in all manner of luxury.

13. Often he went on a pleaſure pillage
To one or another neighboring village,
And moſtly where he was likely to find
Some fair one ſociably inclined.

14. To breaking windows nightly he was addicted,
Many tricks on young *foxes* inflicted,
Dice and cards and billiards played,
And not much progreſs in learning made.

15. In rows and riots he found great enjoyment,
Sleeping in taverns was his daily employment,
But twice in every month or ſo,
To college hall for a change would go.

16. Whenever impatient duns came after
Their money, they were ſent off with laughter,
Or elſe in counterfeit money were paid,
And very angry and fooliſh made.

17. His books and clothes he'd ſell to pawnbrokers
And ſpend the money with drinkers and ſmokers,
In ſhort there was none of his time could be
Compared with him in deviltry.

18. To be ſure he was often ſhut up in the Carcer,
And there to the law was made to anſwer,
And for his crimes on one occaſion
He barely eſcaped the relegation.

19. For three years long he had purſued this vocation,
And often for money had made application
To his parents, but his letters were worded ſo
That they never ſuſpected their ſon was ſuch a go.

20. That no one in this could poſſibly be apter
Than Hieronimus we ſhall ſhow in the next chapter,
Which gives of this queer correſpondence a taſte,
And therefore now cloſe the preſent in haſte.

Notes.

Stanza 7. *In Floribus*, equivalent to our "living in clover."

Stanza 8. "Let us then rejoice while our youth is blooming!"

Stanza 11. *Pereat*! is the oppoſite of *Vivat*!

Stanza 14. *Foxes* are freſhmen.

Stanza 18. The Carcer is the college priſon. *Relegation* is diſmiſſal.

CHAPTER XIV.

Contains the copy of a letter, which, among many others, the student Hieronimus did write to his parents

DEAR and Honored Parents,
I lately
Have suffered for want of money greatly;
Have the goodness, then, to send without fail
A trifle or two by return of mail.

2. I want about twenty or thirty ducats;
For I have not at preſent a cent in my pockets;
Things are ſo tight with us this way,
Send me the money at once, I pray.

3. And everything is growing higher,
Lodging and waſhing and lights and fire,
And incidental expenſes every day—
Send me the ducats without delay.

4. You can hardly conceive the enormous expenſes
The college impoſes, on all pretences,
For text-books and lectures ſo much to pay—
I wiſh the ducats were on their way!

5. I devote to my ſtudies unremitting attention—
One thing I muſt not forget to mention:
The thirty ducats—pray ſend them ſtraight
For my purſe is in a beggarly ſtate.

6. Boots and ſhoes, and ſtockings and breeches,
Tailoring, waſhing, and extra ſtitches,
Pen, ink and paper, are all ſo dear!
I wiſh the thirty ducats were here!

7. The money—(I truſt you will ſpeedily ſend it!)
I promise faithfully to ſpend it;
Yes, dear parents, you never need fear,
I live very ſtrictly and frugally here.

8. When other ſtudents revel and riot,
I ſteal away into perfect quiet,
And ſhut myſelf up with my books and light
In my ſtudy-chamber till late at night.

9. Beyond the needful ſupply of my table,
I ſpare, dear parents, all I am able;
Take tea but rarely, and nothing more,
For ſpending money afflicts me ſore.

10. Other ſtudents, who'd fain be called *mellow*,
Set me down for a niggardly fellow,
And ſay: there goes the *dig*, juſt look!
How like a parſon he eyes his book!

11. With jibes and jokes they daily beſet me,
But none of theſe things do I ſuffer to fret me;
I ſmile at all they can do or ſay—
Don't forget the ducats, I pray!

12. Ten hours each day I ſpend at the college,
Drinking at the fount of knowledge,
And when the Lectures come to an end,
The reſt in private ſtudy I ſpend.

13. The Profeſſors expreſs great gratification,
Only they hope I will uſe moderation,
And not wear out in my ſtudiis
Philoſophicis et theologicis.

14. It would ſavor, dear parents, of ſelf-laudation,
To enter on an enumeration
Of all my ſtudies—in brief, there is none
More exemplary than your dear ſon.

15. My head ſeems ready to burſt aſunder,
Sometimes, with its learned load, and I wonder
Where ſo much knowledge is packed away:
(Apropos! don't forget the ducats, I pray!)

16. Yes, dearest parents, my devotion to study
Consumes the best strength of mind and body,
 And generally even the night is spent
 In meditation deep and intent.

17. In the pulpit soon I shall take my station,
And try my hand at the preacher's vocation,
 Likewise I dispute in the college-hall
 On learned subjects with one and all.

18. But don't forget to send me the ducats,
For I long so much to replenish my pockets;
 The money, one day shall be returned
 In the shape of a son right wise and learn'd.

19. Then my *Privatissimum* (I've been thinking on it
For a long time—and in fact begun it)
 Will cost me twenty Rix-dollars more,
 Please send with the ducats I mentioned before.

20. I also, dear parents, inform you sadly,
I have torn my coat of late, very badly,
 So please enclose with the rest in your note
 Twelve dollars to purchase a new coat.

21. New boots are also necessary,
Likewise my night-gown is ragged, very;
 My hat and pantaloons, too, alas!
 And the rest of my clothes are going to grass.

22. Now, as all these things are needed greatly,
Please enclose me four Louis d'ors separately,
 Which, joined to the rest, perhaps will be
 Enough for the present emergency.

23. My recent ſickneſs you may not have heard of,
In fact, for ſome time, my life was deſpaired of,
But I haſte to aſſure you, on my word,
That now my health is nearly reſtored.

24. The Medicus, for ſervices rendered,
A bill of eighteen guilders has tendered,
And then the apothecary's will be,
In round numbers, about twenty-three.

25. Now that phyſician and apothecary
May get their dues, it is neceſſary
Theſe forty-one guilders be added to the reſt,
But, as to my health, don't be diſtreſſed.

26. The nurſe would alſo have ſome compenſation,
Who attended me in my critical ſituation,
I, therefore, think it would be beſt
To encloſe ſeven guilders for her with the reſt.

27. For citrons, jellies and things of that nature,
To ſuſtain and ſtrengthen the feeble creature,
The confectioner, too, has a ſmall account,
Eight guilders is about the amount.

28. Theſe various items, of which I've made mention,
Demand immediate attention;
For order, to me, is very dear,
And I carefully from debts keep clear.

29. I alſo rely on your kind attention,
To forward the ducats of which I made mention
So ſoon as it can poſſibly be—
One more ſmall item occurs to me:—

30. Two weeks ago I unluckily ftumbled,
And down the length of the ftairway tumbled,
As in at the college door I went,
Whereby my right arm almoft double was bent.

31. The Chirurgus who attended on the occafion,
For his balfams, plafters and preparation
Of fpirits, and other things needlefs to name,
Charges 12 dollars; pleafe forward the fame.

32. But, that your minds may be acquiefcent,
I am, thank God, now convalefcent;
Both fhoulder and fhin are in a very good way,
And I go to lecture every day.

33. My ftomach is ftill in a feeble condition,
A circnmftance owing, fo thinks the phyfician,
To fitting fo much, when I read and write,
And ftudying fo long and fo late at night.

34. He, therefore, earneftly advifes
Burgundy wine, with nutmeg and fpices,
And every morning, inftead of tea,
For the ftomach's fake to drink fangaree.

35. Pleafe fend, agreeably to thefe advices,
Two piftoles for the wine and fpices,
And be fure, dear parents, I only take
Such things as thefe for the ftomach's fake.

36. Finally, a few fmall debts, amounting
To thirty or forty guilders (loofe counting),
Be pleafed, in your letter, without fail,
Dear parents, to enclofe this bagatelle.

37. And could you, for ſundries, ſend me twenty
Or a dozen Louis d'or (that would be plenty),
'Twould be a kindneſs ſeaſonably done,
And very acceptable to your ſon.

38. This letter, dear parents, comes hoping to find you
In uſual health—I beg to remind you
How much I am for money perplexed,
Pleaſe, therefore, to remit in your next.

39. Herewith I cloſe my letter, repeating
To you and all my friendly greeting,
And ſubſcribe myſelf, without further fuſs,
Your obedient ſon,
HIERONIMUS.

40. I add in a poſtſcript what I neglected
To ſay, beloved and highly reſpected
Parents, I beg moſt filially,
That you'll forward the money as ſoon as may be.

41. For I had, dear father (I ſay it weeping),
Fourteen French Crowns laid by in ſafe keeping
(As I thought) for a day of need—but the whole
An anonymous perſon yeſterday ſtole.

42. I know you'll make good, unaſked, each ſhilling,
Your innocent ſon has loſt by this villain;
For a man ſo conſiderate muſt be aware
That I ſuch a loſs can nowiſe bear.

43. Meanwhile I'll take care that, to-day or to-morrow,
Mifter Anonymous fhall, to his forrow
And your fatisfaction, receive the reward
Of his gracelefs trick with the hempen cord.

Note.

Stanza 19. In college, purfuing an extra ftudy with fome Tutor is called taking a *private;* of courfe a *privatiffimum* would be a *very* private courfe. See "College Words and cuftoms."

CHAPTER XV.

Here follows a copy of the written reply of old Senator Jobs to the foregoing letter.

OLD Senator Jobs's anſwer (*verbatim,*
Literatim atque punctatim)
In form and manner as follows would run:
Dearly beloved and hopeful ſon!

2. I am very happy to ſee, by thy letter,
That thy health and proſpects are daily better,
Neverthele ſs it cauſes me pain,
That thou makeſt mention of money again.

3. It is ſcarce three months, O rareſt of ſcholars!
Since I ſent thee a hundred and fifty dollars,
I wonder, my ſon, thou conſidereſt not
Where in the world ſo much caſh can be got.

4. I alſo learn, with lively ſatisfaction,
That thou findeſt in ſtudy ſuch great attraction,
But it is with the higheſt concern I ſee
That thou aſkeſt thirty ducats of me.

5. Allow me, my ſon, the obſervation,
That, on the moſt liberal computation,
A univerſity reſidence
Cannot be, with frugality, ſuch an expenſe.

6. Moſt truly thou art right in ſaying
That lectures and books are not had without paying,
But it muſt take a great many to come
To ſuch an enormons, unheard-of ſum.

7. For lodging and waſhing and lights and fire
One cannot poſſibly require
So much, and for paper and pens and ink
A very few pence would ſuffice, I ſhould think.

8. I alſo perceive with gratification
That thou keepeſt thyſelf from the contamination
Of evil companions, eſpecially by night,
Thy books and chamber thy ſole delight.

9. Likewise I am greatly pleaſed with thy drinking
Nothing but tea,—but I can't help thinking:
To one who pores over his books and drinks tea,
What uſe can theſe thirty ducats be?

10. That other ſtudents for a niggard abuſe thee
May very properly amuſe thee,
For he who ſpends all that thou haſt figured,
Deſerves to be called anything but a niggard.

11. Let me adviſe thee to continue the attention
To thy ſtudies of which thou makeſt mention,
That thy precious time and thy money, both,
May be wiſely ſpent and not waſted in ſloth.

12. But mind, my ſon, the advice of the phyſician,
And beware of even a *laudable* ambition,
For alas! too often we find it a rule
That the greateſt ſcholar's the greateſt fool.

13. Thy purpose of preaching deſerves commendation,
Be diligent, therefore, in thy preparation,
But from much diſputation, when all is done,
Precious little wiſdom comes out, my ſon.

14. The uſe of a *Privatissimum* I can't conjecture,
When one is already ten hours at lecture,
And I comprehend it the leſs, as you ſay,
There are twenty Rixdollars to pay.

15. But I waive all further commentary,
For the money thou findeſt neceſſary
In purſuing thy ſtudies I gladly allow,
And though it were three times as much as now.

16. According to thy ſtory (no doubt a true one),
Thou haſt torn thy coat, and need'ſt a new one,
Nevertheleſs the cloth muſt be ſuperfine,
To coſt twelve dollars, or even nine.

17. But he that will ſtudy to be a paſtor,
Should not dreſs ſo much better than his Maſter,
Therefore a ſomewhat coarſer ſtuff
Would make thee a coat quite good enough.

18. For other articles of wearing apparel
About the four Louis d'or, I shan't quarrel,
When night-gown, hat and trowſers wear out,
New ones are neceſſary without doubt.

19. But if I muſt make, for all this raiment,
And ſo forth, ſpecial and ſeparate payment,
What ſhall become, Hieronimus dear,
Of the thirty ducats, to me is not clear.

20. I received with much feeling the information
Of thy recent critical ſituation,
But to tamper with phyſic to ſuch an extent,
I muſt ſay, my ſon, is money miſpent.

21. For I ſcarce ever knew of the rule failing,
With young folks eſpecially, that when one is ailing,
Nature does better when left to herſelf,
Than the beſt mixture on the apothecary's ſhelf.

22. The expenſe of the Doctor and his preparation
Seems to me little leſs than an abomination,
And I very ſeriouſly queſtion:
Can an apothecary or a Doctor be a Chriſtian?

23. And as to the nurſe's compenſation
Who attended you in your critical ſituation,
'Twould have been enough if thou hadſt given
A ſingle guilder inſtead of ſeven.

24. Unleſs ſhe had previouſly ſhown thee attention
Of another deſcription which thou doſt not mention,
For this, dear ſon, I am forced to infer,
From thy paying ſeven guilders to her.

25. And then the confectioner's bill of eight guilders—
My ſon, my ſon! it almoſt bewilders
Thy father's brain!—if thou hadſt been wiſe,
A dollar at moſt would now ſuffice.

26. For citrons, confits, and things of that nature,
Adminiſter no ſtrength to the feeble creature,
But oatmeal gruel and barley drinks
Are better, far, for the ſick, methinks.

27. To fall down ſtairs is highly injurious,
See to it next time thou art not ſo furious
To get to thy ſtudies, but take more care,
For it coſts a great deal ſuch damage to repair.

28. Thy ſurgeon has taken thee in completely,
For our town-barber, who works ſo neatly,
Will, for twelve dollars, I'm told, reſtore
A broken leg as whole as before.

29. But I'm happy to hear of thy reſtoration,
For when the parſon is in his peroration,
His arm muſt be in a flexible ſtate,
That ſo he may pound and geſticulate.

30. I muſt further lament thy ſtomach's weakneſs
Occaſioned by thy recent ſickneſs;
My ſtomach, I'm ſorry to ſay, is feeble
From ſitting ſo much at the Council-table.

31. Neverthel͏eſs my earneſt advice is:
Abſtain from Burgundy wine and ſpices;
A bit of flag-root now and then
Will help thy ſtomach as much again.

32. Thou mentioneſt "ſome ſmall debts, amounting
To thirty or forty guilders, (looſe counting);"
I've thought and thought and racked my brain
To gueſs what debts thoſe can be, but in vain.

33. Thou haſt given already in ſpecification,
Item by item (outſide calculation),
And forty guilders, thou knoweſt full well,
Upon my ſoul are no "bagatelle!"

34. And finally thou needeſt (for ſuch thy pretence is),
A dozen Piſtoles for thy general expenſes;
No doubt it were very agreeable to thee,
But to me inconvenient in the higheſt degree.

35. For as to any unexpected urgency
Thoſe *thirty ducats* will meet the emergency,
Theſe laſt dozen Louis d'or ſeem to me,
In that view, a mere ſuperfluity.

36. And as to the ſtolen crowns, thy ſuggeſtion,
In point of delicacy, admits of a queſtion,
For truly the reparation were ſorer to me
Than the alleged robbery is to thee.

37. But, from this diſagreeable ſubject to paſs on,
Thy propoſal to ſtring the thief up ſans façon
Is by no means a Chriſtian ſentiment;
Mr. Anonymous may one day repent.

38. Beſides, 'tis a matter of congratulation
In theſe our days of illumination,
I ſay it confidentially in thy ear,
Holy juſtice has grown leſs ſevere.

39. No one who chances a drawer to rifle,
Need mount the double ladder for ſuch a trifle,
At leaſt, in our wiſe Schildburg they ſay,
Far greater rogues go clear every day.

40. When thou in future haſt money in keeping,
I adviſe thee to guard it with vigilance unſleeping,
For nothing is ſo univerſal a ſubject of ſpeculation
As money depoſited for preſervation.

41. I and thy mother underſtand the thing better,
Learn wiſdom, therefore, from this preſent letter
We always lock our caſh up tight
And anxiouſly watch it by day and night.

42. But to appeaſe thy preſent deſire,
And ſupply what immediate wants require,
Be pleaſed hereby the moneys to find
In a ſealed linen bag, each ſeparate kind.

43. Neverthelefs, I muſt hint to thee, Hieronimus,
That the times we live in are rather ominous,
And it coſts me many an anxious thought
Where ſo much money can ever be got.

44. There's a very ſmall trifle of buſineſs doing,
Folks are ſo poor—ſcarce anything brewing
In the honorable Council, and ſo
My incomes, you ſee, are very low.

45. I ſhall, therefore, await with pleaſed expectation,
The day of thy final graduation,
Eſpecially as, by this time, without doubt,
Thou haſt in every branch learned out.

46. For if thou ſhould'ſt longer ſtay and ſtudy
As diligently and *dearly* as thou haſt already,
I ſhall grow as poor as Job was once,
Utterly unable to raiſe any more funds.

47. We all deſire to welcome, greatly,
Our learned ſon in a ſtyle right ſtately,
Eſpecially thy mother with joy
Looks forward to the return of her boy.

48. I wiſh I had ſome news to write you,
But things are moſtly in *quo ſita*;
I go as uſual, early and late,
To the Council-room to deliberate.

49. There we have had in conſideration,
In pleno, many an alteration,
Whereby our police affairs may be
Adminiſtered judiciouſly.

50. Thy mother's teeth have troubled her greatly,
But a diſtinguiſhed ſurgeon, lately,
From foreign parts, came along one day,
And took the troubleſome teeth away.

51. A perſon is paying attention to your ſiſter
Gertrude, his name and title is Miſter
Procurator Geier, 'tis well under way,
And Trudy grows taller every day.

52. Our old parſon is always ailing,
They think his health is decidedly failing,
If this excellent man ſhould be taken away,
Thou mighteſt be our Parſon one day.

53. Our wealthy neighbor's daughter Betty
Sends hearty greetings—the girl is pretty,
And neat and tidy, and would be
A nice little parſon's wife for thee.

54. Thy brothers and ſiſters all ſend their greeting
In the joyful hope of a ſpeedy meeting,
They are glad to hear of thy health and ſucceſs,
And, with wiſhes for thy happineſs,

55\. I remain,
Thy father (in courſe of natur),
Hans Jobs, *pro tempore* Senater.
P. S. Write again at an early day,
But ſpare thy alluſions to money, I pray.

Notes.

Stanza 40. Does not the laſt couplet ſeem almoſt prophetic?

Stanza 43. N. B.—The rhyme in the firſt couplet is ſtrictly copy-righted.

Stanza 48. The ſecond line ſhows old Jobs a rare Latiniſt.

Stanza 49. In pleno—or, as *we* might ſay, "in Committee of the Whole."

CHAPTER XVI.

How Hieronimus finiſhed his ſtudies, and how he journeyed home, and how it ſtood with his learning; neatly repreſented in the preſent engraving.

SINCE, now, one cannot forever tarry
At univerſities, it became neceſſary
That after a ſpace of three years had flown
Hieronimus ſhould prepare to go home.

2. As his time of ſtudy had now fully expired
And his preſence at home was very much deſired,
Immediately he ſet about
Doing all that was needed to fit himſelf out.

3. His luggage required but a ſhort time to pack it
For ſaving boots, ſword, waiſtcoat and jacket,
And whatever elſe on his body was ſeen,
There was no other article, dirty or clean.

4. For books there was no need of aſking about them,
He could get along very well without them,
And except a ſingle ſermon alone
Not the leaſt ſcripture did he own.

5. A friend had given him this as a preſent,
And taught him to repeat it by labour inceſſant,
That ſo, whenever an occaſion tranſpired,
He might preach eaſily at home if deſired.

6. He thought with no little trepidation
Of preſenting himſelf to his parents in this ſituation,
For if in this manner he ſhould appear,
The ſtate of the caſe would at once be clear.

7. At laſt he concluded, that when they began to
Inquire about his purſe and portmanteau,
He would make believe that ſomebody ſtole,
On his journey home, the whole.

8. Alſo ſome ſighs would ſtart, quite ominous,
How will it fare with thee, poor Hieronimus!
When thou an examination ſhalt undergo,
And ſhow how much thou doſt not know?

9. Verily he was filled with remorſe and vexation
So that he almoſt ſhed tears on the occaſion,
To think that for ſo much time and coſt
He had ſo little learning to boaſt.

10. But all his manœuvering, contriving and inventing,
Wiſhing and ſighing and groaning and grunting,
Brought him no ſort of peace at all,
For the time was gone beyond recall.

11. Therefore, by way of alleviation,
He ſent out formaliter an invitation
To his friends at the univerſity,
And gave them a valedictory ſpree.

12. Here then, once more, was a regular rollicking,
Drinking and ſmoking and ſinging and frolicking,
'Till at laſt the diſmal morning breaks,
And Hieronimus his farewell takes.

13. Right heavily now his heart was ſhaken
And bitter grief did the parting awaken,
Yes, he really boohoo'd right out
In the arms of the friends that crowded about.

14. Before, however, his final clearance,
At the Profeſſor's he made his appearance,
Who gave him, for the ready money,
An academic teſtimony.

15. It was not indeed quite creditable,
But Hieronimus, who to read it was unable,
(For it was written in Latin and Greek)
Into his bag the paper did ſtick.

16. We leave him, therefore, his journey purſuing
Homeward, the reader meanwhile may be viewing,
Prefixed to this chapter, a copper-plate
That ſhows, as to learning, his real ſtate.

CHAPTER XVII.

How Hieronimus, booted and ſpurred, returns to his friends.

ONE day, when old Senator Jobs, after dinner,
(For ſuch was his accuſtomed manner,)
With pipe in mouth, leaned back his head
In the eaſy-chair and his newſpaper read;

2. And meanwhile, Mrs. Jobs was making a pother
In the kitchen, about ſomething or other,
And nobody dreaming of any harm,
All on a ſudden there roſe an alarm;

3. For a ſtately rider, booted and ſpurry,
Came riding up the ſtreet in a hurry,
And ſtraight at the houſe they heard, ſlam-bang,
Somebody diſmount with a terrible clang.

4. Like a knell in the ſamily's ears it ſounded,
Old Jobs let fall his paper, aſtounded,
And the pipe itſelf came near to break;
And Mrs. Jobs was too frightened to ſpeak.

5. But ſoon from this panic in which they were taken,
The rider did their ſenſes 'waken,
As, in full traveling coſtume,
He came at once right into the room.

6. The old folks apparently neither of them knew him,
But he kept quiet and let them view him,
Till at laſt the old man jumped from his chair
To ſee his dear Hieronimus there.

7. I have not the qualifications in any meaſure,
To ſing the exceeding and mighty pleaſure
Of the good old Senator at ſeeing his boy,
He almoſt went out of his head for joy.

8. The mother too, could hardly contain herſelf,
Nor from kiſſing his hands and feet reſtrain herſelf,
As ſoon as ſhe ſaw that it muſt needs be
Hieronimus, and none but he.

9. They almoſt cried, in the overmeaſure
Of their very great and diſtreſſing pleaſure,
And the Welcome home! and the God be praiſed!
Held on till a ſtranger had been half-crazed.

10. And Senator Jobs's remaining children
Were alſo at hand, till it became quite bewilderin',
They all of them ſeemed in a perſect bother,
For not a ſoul of them knew their brother.

11. 'Twas really exceeding curious
To hear what the children made of Hieronimus:
One held him to be a diſtinguiſhed gueſt
Who had juſt arrived from the Eaſt or Weſt;

12. Another, on account of his ſword and his danger-
ous dreſs and equipment, conſidered the ſtranger
As one who bags up children ſmall;
This thought did the youngeſt particularly appal.

13. But very funny was it with Eſther,
Our Hieronimus's youngeſt ſiſter,
For ſhe kept up a continual clack
About her ſtrange uncle from Gengenbach.

14. In the three years he had ſpent at college,
His perſon had quite outgrown their knowledge,
His belly had waxed exceeding thick
And there was a deal of hair on chin and cheek.

15. It was not, therefore, a matter of wonder
That they at firſt ſhould make ſuch a blunder,
Eſpecially as his ſtudent-dreſs
Made it difficult, who he was, to gueſs.

16. A very tall hat with a very tall feather,
Breeches and waiſtcoat of yellow buck's leather,
With a ſhort cravat of ſome gray ſtuff,
Diſguiſed Hieronimus well enough.

17. Add to this a mighty great ſword, ſuſpended
From his left ſide, with which he defended
His perſon from any ſudden attack,
Fit alike for a thruſt or a thwack.

18. And then his look, ſo martial and bloody,
That ſeemed to threaten death to everybody;
His hair hanging down in great maſſes too,
And behind, a great pig-tail of a queue.

19. Theſe and other arrangements I might mention,
Soon attracted his father's attention,
For a ſimple decorous black dreſs
Would better have ſuited his parents, I gueſs.

20. Nor did Hieronimus's general behaviour
Recommend him to old father Jobs's favour,
Eſpecially when he Hieronimus heard
Venting curſes at every word.

21. He gave him, therefore, to underſtand clearly
That he muſt alter all this entirely,
For ſurely a young Theologus
Muſt never be heard to ſwear and cuſs.

22. When a few moments after he aſked for the coffer,
Hieronimus did the information proffer,
And ſwore to it moſt luſtily:
It was ſtolen from the poſtwagon, ſaid he.

23. This diſagreeable information
Threw the father into great agitation,
And he would immediately have begun
To ſcold, but the mother excuſed her ſon;

24. Sne ſtepped between Hieronimus and his father,
Saying, 'tis ſurely the misfortune rather
  Than any fault of our dear ſon;
  So the old man ſubmitted and was mum.

25. Meanwhile the neighbours were rapidly learning
The news of Hieronimus's returning,
  From houſe to houſe the rumour flew
  'Till it was known the whole town through.

26. It ſeemed a weighty public matter,
It kept the ſtreets in a conſtant clatter,
  And at every caſual neighborly meeting
  "Hieronimus is here" was the very firſt greeting.

27. In univerſal congratulation,
At Senator Jobs's habitation,
  The reſt of the remaining day did wag
  And nothing more was thought of the bag.

28. Hieronimus feaſted away quite cheery,
For his journey had made him faint and weary,
  And he ſmoked till he emptied, as I can vouch,
  His daddy's great tobacco pouch.

NOTE.

In the wood-cut that heads this Chapter, the object on the left reſembling a ſcrew, as if to draw the rider along by an inviſible wire, is preſumed to be no more nor leſs than a mile-ſtone. The reader will pleaſe not let it diſturb his dreams.

CHAPTER XVIII.

How Hieronimus now began to be clerical, and how he got a black dreſs and a peruke, and how he preached for the firſt time in the pulpit, &c.

THE day after that to which we've been referring,
When all in the houſe were up and ſtirring,
And round the breakfaſt table they ſat,
Sipping their coffee in ſocial chat,

2. The father began to call attention
As follows: Dear Son, it is proper to mention,
That thy ſtyle of raiment hitherto
Will for the future hardly do.

3. And firſt and foremoſt muſt thou haſten
That terrible ſword from thy ſide to unfaſten,
Becauſe a ſervant of the Lord
Don't never fight except with the word.

4. Likewiſe the gray collar and waiſtcoat of leather
And breeches and boots muſt be laid aſide altogether,
As alſo the mighty feather hat,
For no clergyman is allowed to wear that.

5. For if this rig ſhould be ſeen by any body,
They would certainly cry out, "O Luddy!
We've ſurely got a cuiraſſier,
Inſtead of our future parſon, here."

6. Know alſo that a round peruke is fitter
For a clerical head and looks much better,
And a great deal more reſpectable, too,
Than ropy hair and a pig-tail queue!

7. It is therefore thy father's pleaſure
That the tailor ſhould come and take thy meaſure,
That he may make thee this very day
A ſuit of black without delay.

8. The peruke-maker has alſo had warning,
To come, if you pleaſe, this very morning,
To make thee a wig that thou mayſt wear
Over thy frowzy head of hair.

9. It will make thee look reſpectable, very,
But it is alſo neceſſary
That thou ſhouldſt leave off ſwearing to-day
And endeavour to live in a clerical way.

10. Hieronimus liſtened, reluctantly rather,
To the rational counſel of his father,
But concluded to fulfil the deſire
Of his grave and venerable ſire.

11. Behold him, therefore, ere the day had expired,
In full black dreſs and peruke attired,
He was alſo in a white cravat arrayed
By his mother's *manu propriâ* made.

12. Thus clerically fitted out, he communicated
To his parents that he meditated,
God willing, in this livery
To preach next Sunday publicly.

13. On the Sunday following Hieron'mus
Did really preach in purſuance of his promiſe,
And without ſpecial obſtacle
Got through his ſermon very well.

14. For as we above, Chapter XVI., made mention,
A friend had politely ſhown him the attention
Of writing for him a ſermon, which he
Could now deliver conveniently.

15. 'Twas an excellent piece of compoſition,
Choke full of wiſdom and erudition,
And ſmelt ſo of the ſtudy ſhelf
That Hieronimus did'nt underſtand it himſelf.

16. His external appearance was likewiſe ſplendid,
His arms and hands he mightily extended,
And his tenor voice ſo ſtrong and clear
Went ſtately into the public ear.

17. His ſermon was heard by many hundred,
Who all at his talent greatly wondered,
They nodded their heads and the whiſper ran
Through all the houſe: "What a wonderful man!

18. "Who on earth would have ever ſuſpected
That anything like this could have been concocted
Out of Jobs's dull Hieronimus?
'Tis a perfect miracle to us!"

19. Likewiſe there was not a ſingle relation
Abſent from the congregation,
And every one thought: "Our couſin Jobs
Looks remarkably well in his clerical robes!"

20. But 'tis vain to attempt to deſcribe the elation
Of the two good parents on this occaſion,
There cannot be a doubt, thought they,
He's the greateſt orator of the day.

21. When divine ſervice had come to a termination,
They adjourned to partake of a great collation,
Given in Senator Jobs's houſe,
Where all the relations went to carouſe.

22. And while the dinner they were eating,
Hieronimus' praiſe they were conſtantly repeating,
And many a great glaſs of wine
Was drunk to the health of our young divine.

23. The whole aſſembly was alſo unanimous
That, under exiſting circumſtances, Hieronimus,
Who to-day had preached ſo brilliantly
Before the preſent company,

24. Muſt certainly next make bold to venture
His name as candidate to enter,
That ſo, in optima formâ he
Should Candidatus Miniſterii be.

25. 'Tis true, as a preliminary,
An Examen would be neceſſary,
But the recent ſpecimen ſhowed that he
Would find therein no difficulty.

26. Eſpecially as the preſent incumbent was weakly,
Old and infirm and ſomewhat ſickly,
Hieronimus might without any offence
Enter the vacant pariſh at once.

27. That is, in caſe, by the bleſſing of heaven,
The parſon ſhould go the way of all living,
For his feeble conſtitution gave place
For ſuſpicion that this would be ſhortly the caſe.

28. Hieronimus, overpowered by the ſolicitations
And weighty reaſons of his friends and relations,
Gave, anxiouſly enough, God knows,
His conſent to what they did propoſe.

29. For the reſt, he emptied with great pleaſure
Of liquor many a brimming meaſure,
But when that Examen came into his head
It ſtruck his heart with a ſort of dread.

30. At laſt his anxiety ſought conſolation
In a regular fit of intoxication,
Although old Jobs his diſpleaſure made known,
By repeatedly ſhaking his head at his ſon.

NOTE.

Stanza 8. *Frowny.* This word is not *frouzy*, which has a different meaning. Our word is found only in an old Dictionary in the Jobs family.

CHAPTER XIX.

How Hieronimus was examined for a Candidate, and how he made out.

HOWEVER he ſtuck to his determination,
And the cleriſy held a convocation,
And every one came in his wig and robes
To the examination of Hieronimus Jobs.

2. But how he felt in view of his danger,
Being to learning an utter ſtranger,
And what an anxious face he made,
The reader will not comprehend, I'm afraid.

3. The ſcene is beyond my power of painting:
If he ever in his life ſaw the hour for fainting,
That hour at laſt was approaching now;
Alas! thou poor Hieronimus, thou!

4. Begin now, Miſs Muſe, an enumeration
Of the clerical gentleman whom the examination
Brought hither on the appointed day
From every quarter of Swabia.

5. The firſt, *that* was the *Herr Inſpector*,
In doctrine ſtrong as a ſecond Hector,
A ſtately, pot-bellied man was he,
Whom you ſaw at a glance an Inſpector to be.

6. This poſt was accorded to his ſingular merit,
Its burdens he bore with a patient ſpirit,
And, to ſay the truth, with a cheerful mood,
And daily ate and drank what was good.

7. And after him came the *ghoſtly Aſſeſſor*,
A man whoſe breadth was ſomewhat leſſer,
But height much greater: he was ſpare of limb,
And his diſpoſition exceedingly grim.

8. He not only the ſpiritual intereſts defended,
But to matters of economy alſo attended,
And drank only bad wine and beer,
For his income was ſmall and his habit ſevere.

9. Then came *Herr Krager*, an oldiſh man rather,
Who was very well verſed in many a church father,
And to prove a point could readily quote
Whatever any one of 'em wrote.

10. Next *Herr Kriſch*, polite as a Caſtilian,
Who was, in Poſtils, a perfect poſtillion;
Poſted up in them as well as the beſt
Parſon the Swabian land poſſeſſed.

11. Next *Herr Beſſ*, a Linguiſt of great reputation,
And a tolerable chriſtian in walk and converſation,
In lecturing a terrible bore,
But always Orthodox to the core.

12. Next *Herr Schrei*, a man of great notoriety
Alike in the pulpit and in general ſociety,
Free and eaſy—had no wife,
And led with his cook an exemplary life.

13. Next *Herr Plotz*, an angelic creature,
In his youth of a ſomewhat genial nature,
But when to preach he once began
He became a very pious man.

14. He kept his belovéd congregation
From vice and evil communication,
Faithful in ſeaſon and out was he
To admoniſh, when he had opportunity.

15. Next *Herr Keffer*, who never could tire
In following his ſheep through mud and mire,
But alas! in his flock, beſide the lambs,
Were likewiſe many ſtiff-necked old rams.

16. Sometimes, to get them to follow his leadings,
He inſtituted legal proceedings,
For he underſtood the jura of the ſtate
As well as the very beſt advocate.

17. Beſides thoſe named in the above enumeration,
Other clerical gentlemen attended the examination,
Whom I neither need nor can
Particularly deſignate man by man.

18. Now when the reverend and ghoſtly faces
Had all come together in their places,
Præmiſſis præmittendis, they
Round a great table ſate ſtraightway.

19. With trembling and quaking came Hieronimus
Before this aſſembly of white bands ſo ominous,
And ſcraped a greeting ſubmiſſively,
Oh, woe, Hieronimus! woe on thee!

20. Firſt and formoſt inquired the *Examinatores*
About his previous manners and *mores*,
And preſently aſked him whether he
Had a certificate from the univerſity?

21. Hieronimus, without heſitation,
Handed the inſpector the atteſtation,
Who read the ſame immediately:
Alas! Hieronimus, woe on thee!

22. 'Tis true, the document was worded,
In Latin and Greek, as above recorded,
And conſequently not eaſy to read,
But unfortunately, as ill luck decreed,

23. The Inſpector made out, in a free tranſlation
To give a ſubſtantial interpretation,
For no other clergyman in the hall
Dared undertake the taſk at all.

24. To leave no breach in this narration,
I will now give the reader full information,
What Hieronimus' certificate,
Word for word, did properly ſtate.

25. Firſt the name and title of the Profeſſors,
And then in larger hand, the letters
L. B. S., and the meaning of them
Was *Lectori Benevolo Salutem!*

26. "Forafmuch as Herr Hieronimus Jobsius
As Theologiæ Studiofus,
During three years' and fome weeks' fpace
Had his refidence in this place,—

27. "And the fame now has it in contemplation
To take his leave, and has made application
For a written certificate to me,
A ftep of great propriety,—

28. "I could not refufe his reafonable defires,
But give hereby the atteft he requires,
That the fame did every quarter of a year
Once at my lecture-room appear.

29. "Whether the reft was devoted to ftudy
Himfelf knows better than anybody,
For I in this official report
Affert and teftify nothing of the fort.

30. "And as to general behaviour,
There is not much to be faid in his favour,
Entire filence on that point would be
The part of chriftian charity.

31. "For the reft I have only to fay, God fpeed him
On his journey home, and may heaven lead him,
When all thefe earthly troubles are paft,
To the place where he belongs at laft!"

32. How the eyes of the learned body diftended
When the reading of this document ended,
And that Herr Hieronimus did not laugh
The reader can imagine readily enough.

33. However on all hands it ſeemed better
For this once to overlook the matter,
And for charity's ſake to find all the good
In the teſtimonial that they could.

34. For the gentlemen wiſely recollected
How many of *their* tricks had not been detected,
And how if they had, it had fared with them,
And ſo they proceeded at once *ad rem.*

35. The Herr Inſpector he led off,
Clearing the way with a mighty cough,
Repeated thrice, thrice did he ſtroke
His portly paunch and then he ſpoke:

36. "I, for the time *pro tempore* Inſpector
And of the clergy preſent Director,
Aſk you: *Quid ſit Epiſcopus?*"
Straightway replied Hieronimus:

37. "A Biſhop is, as I conjecture,
An altogether agreeable mixture
Of ſugar, pomegranate juice and red wine,
And for warming and ſtrengthening very fine."

38. The Candidate Jobs this anſwer making,
There followed of heads a general ſhaking!
And firſt the Inſpector ſaid, hem! hem!
Then the others *ſecundum ordinem.*

39. And now the *Aſſeſſor* began to inquire:
"*Herr Hieronimus! tell me, I deſire,
Who the Apoſtles may have been?*"
Hieronimus quick made anſwer again:

40. "Apoſtles they call great jugs, I'm thinking,
In which wine and beer are kept for drinking,
In the villages, and from them oft
By thirſty Burſchés liquor is quaffed."

41. The Candidate Jobs this anſwer making,
There followed of heads a general ſhaking,
And firſt the Inſpector ſaid, hem! hem!
Then the others *ſecundum ordinem.*

42. Herr Krager now in his turn ſtood ready:
And "*if you pleaſe, Herr Candidate,*" ſaid he,
"*Inform me who was St. Auguſtin?*"
Hieronimus anſwered with open mien:

43. "The only Auguſtine of whom I've any knowledge
Is the one I uſed to know at college,
Auguſtine, the beadle of the univerſity,
Who often before the Prorector cited me."

44. The Candidate Jobs this anſwer making,
There followed of heads a general ſhaking,
And firſt the Inſpector ſaid hem! hem!
Then the others *ſecundum ordinem.*

45. Now followed Herr Kriſch at once and requeſted
To know "*of how many parts a ſermon conſiſted,*
In other words, how many diviſions muſt there be,
When it is written ruleably?" ſaid he.

46. Hieronimus having taken a moment to determine,
Replied; "There are two parts to every ſermon:
The one of theſe two parts no man
Can underſtand, but the other he can."

47. The Candidate Jobs this anſwer making,
There followed of heads a general ſhaking,
And firſt the Inſpector ſaid hem! hem!
Then the others *ſecundum ordinem.*

48. Herr Beff the Linguiſt continued the examination,
And deſired of Herr Hieronimus information:
"*What the Hebrew Kibbutz might be?*"
Hieronimus's anſwer was ſomewhat free:

49. "I find in a book to which I've paid attention,
Sophia's tour from Memel to Saxony, mention,
That ſhe to the ſurly Kibbutz fell
Becauſe ſhe refuſed the rich old ſwell."

50. The Candidate Jobs this anſwer making,
There followed of heads a general ſhaking,
And firſt the Inſpector ſaid hem! hem!
Then the others *ſecundum ordinem.*

51. Next in turn it came to Herr Schreier,
Who did of Hieronimus inquire,
"*How many claſſes of angels he
Conſidered there might properly be?*"

52. Hieronimus anſwered, "He never pretended
With all the angels to be acquainted,
But there was one of them he knew
On the Angel-Tavern ſign, painted blue."

53. The Candidate Jobs this anſwer making,
There followed of heads a general ſhaking,
And firſt the Inſpector ſaid hem! hem!
And the others *ſecundum ordinem.*

54. Herr Plotz proceeded with the interrogation:
"*Can you give, Herr Candidate, an enumeration*
Of the concilia œcumenica?"
And Hieronimus anſwered! "Sir,

55. "When I at the univerſity did ſtudy
I was often cited before a body
Called a council, but it never ſeemed to me
To have anything to do with economy."

56. The Candidate Jobs this anſwer making,
There followed of heads a general ſhaking,
And firſt the Inſpector ſaid, hem! hem!
Then the others *ſecundum ordinem.*

57. Then followed his ſpiritual lordſhip, Herr Keffer,
The queſtion he ſtarted ſeemed ſomewhat tougher,
It related "*to the Manichean hereſy*
And what their faith was originally."

58. Anſwer: "Yes theſe ſimple devils
Did really think that without any cavils,
Before my departure, I ſhould pay them off
And in fact I did cudgel them ſoundly enough."

59. The Candidate Jobs this anſwer making,
There followed of heads a general ſhaking,
And firſt the Inſpector said, hem! hem!
Then the others *ſecundum ordinem.*

60. The remaining queſtions that received attention
For want of room I omit to mention;
For otherwiſe the protocol
Would exceed ſeven ſheets, if given in full.

61. For there were many queftions, dogmatical,
Polemical and hermeneutical,
To which Hieronimus made reply
In the manner above, fucceffively.

62. And likewife many queftions in philology
And other fciences ending in *ology*,
And whatever elfe to a clergyman may
Be put on examination day.

63. When the Candidate Jobs his anfwer was making,
There would follow of heads a general fhaking,
And firft the Infpector would fay hem! hem!
Then the others, *fecundum ordinem*.

64. Now when the examination had expired,
Hieronimus by permiffion retired,
That the cafe might be viewed on every fide,
And the council carefully decide:

65. If concience would advife the admiffion
Of Hieronimus to the pofition
And clafs of candidates for the
Holy Gofpel miniftry.

66. Immediately they proceeded to voting,
But very foon, without much difputing,
The meeting was unanimous
That, under the circumftances, Hieronimus

67. Would not perfift in his application
As a candidate for ordination,
But for fpecial reafons they thought it beft,
To let the matter quietly reft.

68. In faſt for years it was kept ſo private,
No ſtranger ever heard anything of it,
But everybody early and late
Held Hieronimus for a candidate.

Notes.

Stanza 48. *Kibbutz* is a corruption for the Hebrew letter Koph.

Stanza 49. Kibbutz is alſo a name for the Owl.

Stanza 57. The German ſtudents nickname their creditors *Manichæans.*

CHAPTER XX.

How the author ſubmiſſively begs pardon, that the former chapter was ſo long, and how he promiſes that the preſent one ſhall be ſo much the ſhorter; a chapter of which the rubric is longer than the chapter itſelf, and which might be omitted without injuring the ſtory.

I HEARTILY beg the reader's pardon,
The previous chapter was ſuch a long and hard one,
The preſent chapter, dear reader, ſhall be
So much the ſhorter, I promiſe thee.

CHAPTER XXI.

How Father Jobs the Senator did deliver Hieronimus a sermon of rebuke, and how he dies of chagrin.

THE reader ſhould have ſeen the conſternation
That roſe in Jobs's habitation,
Becauſe the Examen did not tranſpire
Entirely in accordance with the general deſire.

2. But what then did Hieronimus's father?
Dear reader! pray aſk me, what didn't he do rather?
He ſeized Hieronimus by the nape
Of the neck, and ſaid to him, "Thou ſcape-

3. "grace! is't for this I ſuch kindneſs have done thee
And laviſhed whole handfulls of money upon thee,
'Till I almoſt myſelf a poor man became,
To reap only mortification and ſhame?

4. "Had'ſt thou but ſtudied with application
And behaved in a manner worthy of approbation,
Thou wouldſt without doubt at this time be
A Candidatus Miniſterii.

5. "And wouldſt get a pariſh ſoon and be famous;
But now thou art only an ignoramus,
Who nothing of theology knows,
And all his life long breadleſs goes.

6. "Thy mother and I were often expreſſing
Our hopes that thou wouldſt be one day a bleſſing
To our old age, but oh, what a cuſs
Thou haſt proved, thou vile Hieronimus!

7. "All that thou uſedſt to write of thy doing,
How many ſtudies thou waſt purſuing,
And that none in diligence equalled thee,—
Was a pack of lies, as I now can ſee.

8. "And all that was ſaid of thy privatiſſimo
And about the ten hours in collegio,
How kind the profeſſors were to thee,
And thy ſolitary drinking of tea;

9. "Item, of all the various learning
With which thy head was in danger of turning,
And thy meditation late at night,
And of other ſimilar things a ſight;

10. "And about thy ſtomach becoming ſo feeble
By bending over the ſtudy table,
The whole of it, as I now find,
Was nothing at all but lies and wind.

11. "Oh that I only had liſtened in ſeaſon
To our good Rector's counſel and reaſon,
Who very clearly intimated to me,
That nothing good could be made of thee.

12. "Then had been ſpared a vaſt deal of money
And many a good round patrimony,
Which thou, good-for-nothing ſcoundrel, I ſay,
At the univerſity haſt tippled away!"

13. Such, as the ſon ſtood trembling before him,
Was the ſermon with which old Jobs did ſcore him,
In fact his anger had riſen ſo quick
That at firſt he came near uſing the ſtick.

14. Meanwhile as ſcolding and getting furious
Is generally to health injurious,
As might be imagined very well,
The good old man into a fever fell.

15. In his well days, when younger and tougher,
Severe attacks of gout he would ſuffer,
His Counſellor's office, good living and ease
Prediſpoſed him to this diſeaſe.

16. But now all at once his pains forſook him,
And in the heart the Podagra took him,
And after four-and-twenty hours
He emigrated from this world of ours.

17. No end was there now to the grieving and groaning,
The houſe all wringing their hands and moaning,
And even Hieronimus's grief
Hardly admitted any relief.

18. The reader, I fear, would ſoon be yawning,
If I ſhould deſcribe theſe ſcenes of mourning
Any farther, I therefore ceaſe
And leave poor old Senator Jobs in peace.

CHAPTER XXII.

How Hieronimus almost became Tutor to a young Baron.

ALTHOUGH a fortnight had now expired
Since Senator Jobs to his rest retired,
The thought of the widow Jobs still ran
At times on her dear departed man.

2. Hieronimus meanwhile took his fodder
Up to this time at the house of his mother,
And would gladly in such idleness
Have passed his entire life, I guess;

3. Had he not received a proposition
To look about for a change in condition,
Whereby he might, in the time to come,
Get his living more properly than at home.

4. For it was all over with the expectation
Of getting, as parson, a situation,
So soon as this most heinous dunce
Had preached in each village his sermon once

5. Since now many men of great importance
Began as tutors to make their fortunes,
It entered into Hieronimus's view
That he would be tutor somewhere, too.

6. And fortune ſeemed not unpropitious
To Hieronimus's wiſhes,
For about two months from that time or three
He heard of a fine opportunity.

7. For a neighboring nobleman, (here nameleſs)
Advertiſed for a tutor of character blameleſs,
Who for low board and 8 guilders ſhould come
And teach the young baron, his only ſon.

8. Religion, morality, five kinds of languages
Reading and writing and ſuch like appendages,
Philoſophy, phyſic, geography,
Arithmetic, hiſtory, poetry.

9. Drawing and dancing and riding and fencing
And other accompliſhments needleſs to mention,
Theſe were the branches, every one
To be taught for 8 guilders to the baron's ſon.

10. The Candidate Hieronimus was deſired
To call on his grace, who at once inquired,
Whether the ſaid Hieronimus was the one
Who for eight guilders would teach his ſon?

11. Hieronimus made anſwer: "Gracious
"Sir, it is exceedingly vexatious
To be a tutor, and eight guilders would be
In my opinion quite a ſmall fee;

12. "However to do your grace a pleaſure,
I will at once fall in with the meaſure,
And ſee forthwith what can be done,
In the way of inſtructing the baron your ſon."

13. And ſo was completed the negotiation,
When, contrary to all expectation,
One little difficulty occurred,
Which may be ſtated in a word:

14. Whether Hieronimus in the things deſired,
Could undergo the examination required,
Which he would be obliged to teach every one,
To the young baron, the nobleman's ſon?

15. But it ſoon appeared indiſputable,
That Hieronimus was not able
Himſelf, to underſtand a ſingle one
Of the things he was to teach the nobleman's ſon.

16. He therefore received a quiet diſmiſſion
And jogged home again in an unpleaſant condition
Of mind, and vented his curſes upon
The tutorſhip and the nobleman's ſon.

17. His grace now right and left inquired
Whether another could poſſibly be hired,
Who for the ſum of eight guilders would come
And teach the young baron, his only ſon.

18. Whether he has found it in his power
To obtain ſuch a perſon up to this hour
For eight guilders, I never could learn,
In fact it's a thing wherewith I've no concern.

CHAPTER XXIII.

How Hieronimus became domestic scribe to an old gentleman, who had a chambermaid, named Amelia; and how he behaved himself well till the following chapter.

AMONG all the sundry and manifold stations
Of those who dwell in these earthly habitations,
Without any doubt we may safely call
The widow's estate the saddest of all.

2. When the man, as the head of the woman, is taken
Away, the whole body appears forsaken
By its natural protector quite,
And nothing in the house goes right.

3. The family is straitened and harassed,
The household economy greatly embarassed,
And all is care and sorrow below
And earth becomes a vale of woe.

4. Poor Mrs. Jobs, alas! was fated
To experience the truth just stated,
For all went crab-wise in the house
And she became as poor as a church mouse.

5. Of courſe Hieronimus made his contribution
To the general ſtock of deſtitution,
For he lived as gentlemen of leiſure do,
Ate well and drank ſtill better, too.

6. Meanwhile ſuch houſekeeping every hour
To the worthy widow grew more and more ſour,
And no one feature in it was wuſs
Than the board of Hieronimus.

7. His own conviction grew daily ſtronger,
That things could not go on ſo much longer,
And he therefore began to look round
To ſee if another opportunity could not be found.

8. As, now, in general, the rogues and the dunces
Find in this world the very beſt chances,
It happened that an opening offered again
For Hieronimus with a nobleman.

9. This gentleman lived on his plantation
In a quiet and retired ſituation,
And there, as a genteel cavalier
Spent his large income with *plaiſir*.

10. He is mentioned, in his youth, as engaging
In the ſeven years' war which then was waging,
But he ſtaid in garriſon moſtly, it is ſuppoſed,
And his perſon was very little expoſed.

11. But he was very glad when the war was over,
Being of peace an exceeding lover,
In fact, as a brave man and wiſe one, too,
He anticipated it, and withdrew.

12. And yet he loved to dwell on the ſtory
Of the battles that had covered him with glory,
And how when once he had bravely fought
In the retreat he was almoſt caught.

13. For the reſt he was a man of ſportive habits,
Shot occaſionally hares and rabbits,
Drank at dinner Burgundy of his own,
And lived without any wife alone.

14. He was, in ſo far, an old bachelor; however
He had in the place of a wife a clever
Chambermaid, who early and late
On his urgent neceſſities did wait.

15. He had gradually as he felt himſelf growing older,
Slipped all care of buſineſs off his ſhoulder,
But he had of ſervant men a pair
Who of all things took faithful care.

16. The one of them was a ſly old foxy,
Steward of the houſe and general proxy,
And the other Mr. Servant, he
Was one they called a ſecretary.

17. The ſteward at the time of which we're ſpeaking,
Still lived and found in his office good picking,
For he took good care of cheſt and ſhelf,
Thought leſs of his maſter and more of himſelf.

18. But the above mentioned ſecretary
They had had, ſome days before, to bury,
Becauſe he was dead, which cauſed there to be
In this weighty office a vacancy.

19. Now the ſteward aforeſaid had long been acquainted
With Hieronimus's parents, and therefore painted,
As a true and accom̀modating man,
Hieronimus in the beſt colors he can.

20. And very earneſtly recommended him,
And ſhortly in perſonâ preſented him
To the damſel and the old gentleman, too,
As the moſt capable ſecretary he knew.

21. The chambermaid found his perſon quite ſtriking,
And took to him conſiderable liking,
She therefore promiſed, faithful and true,
To ſpeak the beſt word for him that ſhe knew.

22. The moment ſhe ſaw him ſhe liked him very
Much better than the previous ſecretary;
For Hieronimus was tall and ſtrong,
But his predeceſſor was lean and long.

23. Since now, the old gentleman, as we made mention,
Honored the damſel with his principal attention,
He with favour her application heard,
And gave Hieronimus a nobleman's word.

24. And further to ſhow him the greater honour,
He invited him the firſt day to dinner,
And then the old gent, when dinner was done,
Said to him in a friendly tone:

25. His duty would conſiſt in attending
To the live ſtock and ſeeing what wanted mending,
And whatever was to be written, he
Would write as private ſecretary.

26. And if now this official duty
Hieronimus did faithfully execute, he
  Would pay him, as a ſalary,
  Forty rix-dollars annually.

27. "If you like theſe conditions (ſaid he,) you can tarry
With me *ſub titulo* houſe-ſecretary,
  And I alſo promiſe you, if true,
  Many additional perquiſites, too;

28. "But never go hazing, now remember,
With the damſel that takes charge of the chamber
  For ſuch proceedings will bring you into diſgrace,
  I tell you dryly to your face.

29. "The late, deceaſed houſe-ſecretary,
Was fond of damſels and young women very,
  And I was very much mortified to find
  That he to my maid was ſecretly inclined.

30. "I ſhould, therefore, at once have caſhiered him
And without ceremony cleared him
  Out, but I ſaw he was weak and ſlim,
  And ſo overlooked the fault in him.

31. "The girl, in truth, is ſly and witty,
But ſomewhat deceitful, more's the pity,
  And indeed I have often ſuſpected that ſhe
  Was given to all ſorts of monkery.

32. "I accidentally fell in with her
Five years ago, as we journeyed together;
  I was pleaſed with the manner of the jade,
  And ſo I took her for my maid.

33. "For the reſt, without a ſingle queſtion,
You will hear now my concluding ſuggeſtion;
For I tell you finally once for all,
Have nothing to do with Amelia at all!"

34. Hieronimus muſt have been half-witted,
Had he not on the conditions above ſubmitted,
Accepted very willingly
The part of private ſecretary.

35. He therefore entered on his office right gaily,
And ſaw to the cows and the fences daily,
And many notes he daily took
And wrote in the memorandum book.

36. For example: packets that came by the ſtages,
Money paid out for servants' wages,
The hares that were ſhot and the turkey cocks,
And when they picked the old gentleman's locks.

37. Or what the houſe advocate got for his pleadings,
Or the judge obtained by extra proceedings,
Or what amount at the market was paid
For butter and cheeſe in lawful trade.

38. Or what Amelia's dreſſes coſt to cut 'em,
Or lengthen 'em out at the top and bottom,
Or widen 'em an inch and a-half,
Or when the cow had had a calf.

39. Or when the worthy damſel had needed
On account of fever to be bleeded,
Or a hen had laid an egg; in ſhort,
All incomes and outgoes of every ſort.

40. And where any letters needed inditing,
The old gentleman, who was no hand at writing,
Threw all upon Hieronimus,
Who managed it all without any fuſs.

41. With the help of Talander he wrote them faſter
And quicker by far than any ſchoolmaſter,
(And ſpent leſs time about them too)
Than any ſchoolmaſter I ever knew.

42. The reſt of the time he ſpent at his leiſure,
Ate and drank and ſlept at pleaſure,
So that he hoped he ſhould never give up,
As long as he lived, this ſecretaryſhip.

NOTE.

Stanza 41. *Talander* was probably ſome well-known author of a "Letter-writer." The original ſimply mentions his *Brieſſteller*.

CHAPTER XXIV.

How curious things befel the Secretary Hieronimus, and he was driven away.

INDULGENT reader! our old forefathers
Were ſurely not dunces above all others,
Far oftener will it rather be found
That they had notions both wiſe and ſound.

2. And many a time we find them giving
To us their poſterity rules of good living,
And proverbs full of excellent ſtuff,
Which prove their wiſdom plainly enough.

3. There is one old proverb much celebrated,
And in all countries circulated,
Of which the truth and certainty lies,
Every day, before everybody's eyes.

4. Namely: "whoever can bear in ſucceſſion
A long unbroken continuation
Of nothing but proſperous days, the ſame
Muſt be gifted with a very ſtrong frame."

5. The truth of this old proverb, thus early,
Will in the preſent chapter clearly
Make itſelf manifeſt to us
In the caſe of Hieronimus.

6. He lived like a prince, as much a ſtranger
To want, as a rat in a well filled manger,
Went early to bed and ſlowly crept
From the feathers on which he ſo coſily ſlept.

7. There was nothing in fact to his comfort wanting;
Only one thing his mind would be haunting,—
The image of the damſel always was nigh,
Whom he daily ogled with loving eye.

8. And in her looks and her whole expreſſion
He thought he was able to read a confeſſion
That ſhe with him, the ſecretary,
Was in love, likewiſe, mortally.

9. And often, too, when he looked more nearly
Into her face and ſtudied it clearly,
It always ſeemed to him more and more,
As if he had ſeen her ſomewhere before.

10. Deſpite the old gentleman's prohibition,
He ventured now on a declaration,
And ſoon the knot of intimacy was tied
As cloſe as if they were bridegroom and bride.

11. But, in the old gentleman's preſence, he never
Seemed to take any notice of her whatever;
And very great care he always took
Not to excite ſuſpicion even by a look.

12. Neverthleſs, when alone together
They had many ſly jokes with one another,
And there paſſed not ſeldom a friendly buſs
'Twixt Amelia and Hieronimus.

13. That ſhe meanwhile the old gentleman flattered
Before his face, it nothing mattered
To the ſecretary, who held her free
For all this empty flattery.

14. In return for all his friendly attention
She gave him gifts too numerous to mention,
Shirts and handkerchiefs, gloves and rings,
Caps and cravats and all ſorts of things.

15. Once, on a time, when he had occaſion
In his regular official vocation,
Some writing for her to deſpatch,
She handed him a firſt-rate watch.

16. He thanked her for it very ſincerely,
But when in his hand he held it more nearly,
He cried: "*Potz tauſend Element!* I'm ſure,
I muſt have ſeen this watch before!"

17. Amelia was ſtartled beyond expreſſion,
But made forthwith a candid confeſſion,
That the watch in queſtion, as a preſent, ſhe
Had received from a ſtudent formerly.

18. "How things do often happen queerly,
We ſee in this inſtance very clearly,"
Replied Hieronimus; "for certainly
That ſtudent you before you ſee."

19. And ſo they both now calculated
That five years back their acquaintance dated,
And the watch that was ſtolen ſo long before
The damſel made a joke of,—— no more.

20. And both of them now made themſelves merry,
And thought the joke was comical very,
That, after travelling ſo far round,
The watch ſhould in the right hands be found,

21. For the reſt there was nothing very ſurpriſing
In the chambermaid's not recognizing
In the ſecretary and candidate,
The ſtudent ſhe met in that diſmal ſtate.

22. This laughable affair, however,
Made them henceforth better friends than evei,
And the flirtation they carried on
Made a perfect fool of the old gentleman.

23. Their intercourſe, in its familiarity,
Soon took on an air of bold hilarity,
Till their courting and coquetting came to be
Almoſt undiſguiſedly free.

24. If the damſel in cellar or garden was working,
Mr. Secretary near ſomewhere was lurking,
In kitchen and chamber and all about
He ſtill tagged after her in-doors and out.

25. And even at night, when ſhe was not fuſſing
About the old man, (for he needed much nurſing),
Hieronimus ſometimes went
On a viſit to her apartmént.

26. Alſo, in writing and noting, to guide him
Amelia conſtantly ſat beſide him,
In fact, whether ſitting or ſtanding, ſhe
Was at his ſide inceſſantly.

27. With many a tit-bit of dainty ſavour
From the old man's table ſhe did him favour,
And was there calve's-head or the like of that,
He always got the marrow and fat.

28. And ſometimes ſhe would bring him, on Sunday,
Privately, from the cellar, a flaſk of Burgundy,
Which Hieronimus would drink
At a couple of ſwigs, and never wink.

29. Thus did the days of the houſe ſecretary,
Hieronimus, glide away, quite merry,
No reverend prelate could poſſibly
Lead a more jolly life than he.

30. But it ſoon appeared that this ſituation
Of things could not be of long duration,
For gradually the tranſaction began
To grow more clear to the old gentleman.

31. And inſtead of laughing, in ſuch caſes,
He now began to make ſour faces,
And he gave them to underſtand clearly enough,
That he would not have any more of this ſtuff.

32. And he added, in a manner not very
Gentle, to Mr. Secretary,
If he did not all intercourſe with Amelia quit,
His walking-ticket he ſoon would get.

33. Hieronimus aſſured him on his honour,
He had not behaved improperly in any manner,
And he would not, if his Highneſs preferred,
Exchange with Amelia another word.

34. "Well! in that caſe, you may tarry
As long as you pleaſe, and be ſecretary
All your life to me," replied
The old gentleman, ſomewhat mollified.

35. Although now, from this time Hieronimus
Carried on his tricks as ſlyly as any mouſe,
With the damſel, by day and night,
And did more diligently than ever write;

36. Nevertheleſs, not many days after,
Occurred an adventure too ſerious for laughter,
When the old gentleman who, it ſeems,
Was troubled with uncomfortable dreams,

37. Roſe and went up, as was his cuſtom,
To call Amelia who nurſed him,
That the damſel by her friendlineſs
Might drive away his ſleepleſſneſs,

38, Lo and behold! a mighty wonder!
For there, by ſome unexpected blunder,
Whom ſhould he, to his amazement, ſee,
But Hieronimus, the ſecretary!

39. *Himmel! tauſend Element! potz donner!*
The old gentleman ſwore in ſome ſuch manner,
And from the houſe, the ſelf ſame night,
Hieronimus was forced to take flight.

40. No begging nor praying the matter mended;
The thing was done and there it ended,
And the old man's wrath was ſuch that the maid
Began herſelf to be afraid.

41. Her cunning flatteries, however,
Did once again for this time ſave her,
But the unlucky candidate
Was paſt all help, 'twas now too late.

NOTE.

Stanza 18. The reader is requeſted to obſerve that in the firſt line *how* qualifies *queerly*.

CHAPTER XXV.

How Hieronimus entered into the ſervice of a pious lady, who was a ſpiritual ſiſter, and had unworthy deſigns upon him, and how he ran away from her.

THE ſhirts, rings and other paraphernalia
Which Hieronimus had received from Amelia
Served for ſome time to keep him free
From the actual clutches of poverty.

2. But when, at laſt, he had ſold and ſquandered
All the good damſel had to him tendered,
Nolens volens, now muſt he,
To eſcape from hunger and miſery,

3. And not to die of abſolute ſtarvation,
Begin to look round for a new occupation,
And his firſt thought, of courſe, was to try to find
Some place of ſervice to ſuit his mind.

4. Now, at a ſolitary caſtle there reſided
A widowed lady who was a decided
Spiritual ſiſter, as we ſay,
She was old and her hair already gray.

5. To praying and ſinging ſhe therefore had taken
And other things which as ſpiritual we reckon,
And ſo a number of years had ſpent
And gained the name of a very great ſaint.

6. Not the leaſt ſhadow of ſin could venture
Among her little houſehold to enter,
She called them together twice a day
Into her parlor to ſing and pray.

7. She puniſhed them for the ſmalleſt violations
Of duty by amiably ſtinting their rations,
She thought much of faſts and pſalmody
And a glaſs of brandy occaſionally.

8. At the ſame time, and with reaſon, thinking
That ſocial was better than ſolitary drinking,
And alſo that in society
One could ſing with greater energy,

9. She had for ſome time been deſiring,
And all the country round inquiring,
To find ſome holy man, that he
Might give her his ſpiritual company.

10. Already had many a godly loafer
Preſented himſelf and made his offer,
To live with her and praiſe and pray
In the moſt approved and orthodox way.

11. But no one as yet had had attraction
Enough to give her ſatisfaction,
For this one ſeemed to her too old,
The other by far too young, he was told;

12. One was too meagre, another too weakly,
One was a cripple or otherwiſe ſickly,
Another was deaf or dumb or blind,
Another a worlding, not at all to her mind.

13. Hieronimus finally ventured therefore
His ſervices to the dame to offer,
As ſpiritual aſſiſtant, and lo and behold!
So ſoon as ſhe ſaw him, his fortune was told.

14. For he was neither meagre nor weakly,
Deaf nor dumb nor blind nor ſickly,
Neither too young nor yet too old,
And his perſon was not uncomely to behold.

15. His ſemi-clerical peruke and garment
Took the old lady's eye in a moment,
And he aſſured her faithfully
That he was no worlding, no, not he.

16. And ſo ſhe gave him an invitation
To make to-day his firſt probation,
And he joined with real, holy glee
The pious pſalmody after tea.

17. He alſo read with edification
A family ſermon to the congregation,
And officiated throughout with ſuch grace,
That the dame commended him to his face.

18. Her ſpiritual zeal grew daily more fervent
Through the labors of this her godly ſervant,
And every day a holier flame
Burned in her ſpiritual frame.

19. She kept the pious young man befide her
In all her actions to counfel and guide her,
 And thus Hieronimus foon became
 A very great favorite of the dame.

20. If, once in a while, fome deviation
Occurred, unworthy of his vocation,
 She overlooked fuch things and would call
 Them human frailties—that was all.

21. She would alfo grant him difpenfations
From the penalties fixed for fuch occafions,
 And at fuch times the daintieft fare
 By way of folace, fell to his fhare.

22. Champagne and chocolate and coffee,
And almond milk and fuch rich ftuff, he
 Got for his beverage every day,
 And lived in an extra-luxurious way.

23. He found, in a word, a high enjoyment
In purfuing fuch a holy employment,—
 Eating and drinking all day long,
 With, occafionally, a fermon or fong.

24. The worft thing was that the pious matron
Kept him tied to the ftrings of her apron,
 For fhe really feemed to think that he
 Was the beau ideal of piety.

25. And when on the fofa he fate befide her,
And read fome book that edified her,
 She would ftroke her pious fheep and fay:
 Bravo! in a very rapturous way.

26. And when they ſang a holy meaſure
Together, ſhe could not contain her pleaſure,
She would throw her arm around his neck,
And ſing, as if her heart would break.

27. This very familiar ſtyle of action,
At laſt revealed the whole tranſaction
To Hieronimus, that the old dame
At ſomething more than ſinging did aim.

28. With ſuch a weighty diſcovery before him,
A violent fit of alarm came o'er him,
And when on the mighty danger he thought
He was almoſt paralyſed on the ſpot.

29. When once recovered from his conſternation,
He thought, with many a tender ſenſation,
Of the bliſs he had taſted formerly
In the fair Amelia's company.

30. She was young and faultleſs and charming,
This one, on the contrary, almoſt alarming,
Gray and toothleſs and yellow of ſkin,
Lean and haggard and ugly as ſin.

31. He ſhould, perhaps, have tutored his fancies
And, adapted himſelf to circumſtances,
And, blinking at all her foibles and flaws,
Taken the old lady as ſhe was;

32. But this did not ſuit his diſpoſition,
So he came away without aſking diſmiſſion,
And left the old lady alone, alas!
With her hymn-book and her brandy-glaſs.

CHAPTER XXVI.

How Hieronimus had a bad and a good adventure, and how, for once in his life, he achieved a wise action.

HIERONIMUS, before he decided
To leave the old widow, had provided
A bag of money, deducting the ſame
From the private treaſury of the dame.

2. For he argued that all his ſinging and praying,
And holy things in ſermons ſaying,
And receiving the old lady's careſſes, too,
Made a fair compenſation no more than his due.

3. And now with the fruits of this handſome pillage
He travelled about from city to village,
And as in this way he wandered round
Full many a jolly landlord he found.

4. And when he found in one place or another
Fine quarters and ſometimes a merry brother,
Or a hoſteſs agreeable in her ways,
He commonly tarried ſeveral days.

5. It happened, however, on one occaſion,
That as he thus wandered for recreation,
Juſt as the ſhades of evening fell
He ſtopped at quite a large hotel.

6. It was the beſt tavern in all Swabia,
No better could be found in the wilds of Arabia;
The hoſt was an honeſt man in his talk
And loved to write with double chalk.

7. Now that ſame day, it did befal ſo,
That two ſtrange gueſts had arrived there alſo,
Who, Hieronimus did gueſs,
Were travelling merchants, by their dreſs.

8. In one of them, at the very firſt entrance,
He would almoſt have ſeen an old acquaintance,
Had not a great plaſter on the place,
Diſguiſed about one-half of his face.

9. Meanwhile the two gentlemen grew quite merry,
And invited Hieronimus to partake of their ſherry,
And very ſoon a friendſhip grew
Between Hieronimus and the two.

10. For the man who had on his face the plaſter,
Was, in telling ſtories, a very great maſter,
Some he made up and others were true;
Hieronimus laughed till he was almoſt blue.

11. Hieronimus, in his turn, freely related
All his adventures and communicated
How very near he recently came
To being decoyed by a widowed dame.

12. There followed, of courſe, a peal of laughter,
And Hieronimus, thereafter,
Proceeded to make the ſtory whole
By telling about the money he ſtole.

13. Now when the day, in a manner ſo cheery,
Had come to a cloſe, Hieronimus, weary
And drunk with wine and laughter, ſaid
Good night and ſtaggered off to bed.

14. But hardly had he ſunk to ſlumber,
When the two gentlemen proceeded to his chamber,
Where they ingeniouſly did hook
The money, and their departure took.

15. Hieronimus, waking late in the morning,
And having of miſchief not the leaſt warning,
Found, as he put his pantaloons on
His pocket empty, the money-bag gone.

16. At firſt he could not believe the tranſaction
A real caſe for a legal action,
He thought it only a piece of fun
Which the two merry merchants had done.

17. But when the hoſt, interrogated
Reſpecting them, communicated
That the two gentlemen went away
Quickly at an early hour of the day;—

18. Then did he begin to make lamentations
And outcries great, and his impatience
Grew to ſuch a pitch that the hair
On his head could be kept with difficulty there.

19. His crying and groaning in ſuch a faſhion,
Soon ſtirred the worthy hoſt to compaſſion,
Who agreed to take only his coat in lieu
Of the money that for board was due.

20. And alſo the advice imparted
That it were well now, if he ſtarted,
  "For without the ready caſh," ſaid he,
  "No ſtranger can find quarters with me."

21. Hieronimus's example teaches how odd is,
In this world, the caprice of the bandaged goddess,
  And how, in a manner unlooked for and ſtrange,
  The luck of mortals will often change.

22. Laſt evening the thought of poverty ſcorning,
Called "Sir" by the landlord, and lo! this morning,
  By the ſame worthy landlord hurled
  Coatleſs and pennileſs out into the world.

23. He could now, as he reſumed his wandering,
On his ſad eſtate at leiſure be pondering,
  And at firſt he almoſt wiſhed himſelf back
  (At the ſpiritual ſiſter's, alack!)

24. But when he thought of her careſſes,
And called up her image in memory's receſſes,
  Such a real horror came over him then,
  That he did not care to go back again.

25. He had now, for ſome days, contrived to baniſh
His hunger with an acorn or turnip or radiſh,
  And like a knight errant had managed to ſtay
  His nature in many a pitiful way.

26. But now, as when the need is higheſt,
The conſolation is apt to be nigheſt,
  So was it in poor Hieronimus's caſe
  The help he required was coming apace.

27. For as, on the fourth afternoon, he was lying
In a wood by the roadſide, he heard a crying
Very loud and piteous indeed,
Which from near by did ſeem to proceed.

28. He ſoon arrived at the ſituation
Whence he had heard the lamentation,
And there, to his very great ſurpriſe,
A harrowing ſpectacle met his eyes:

29. A carriage with four horſes ſtopping;
A bearded coachman powerleſs dropping;
There a young lady, who ſhrieked and cried,
And ran deſpairing from ſide to ſide.

30. And here a richly dreſſed gentleman, ſtriving
To keep off two ruffians who at him were driving,
And who were ſeeking with might and main,
To give him his *quietus*, 'twas plain.

31. My hero recognized at ſome diſtance,
The *quaſi* merchants, his tavern acquaintance,
He therefore lifted his ſtick, and flew
At once, like a fury, upon the two.

32. "Villains! where is my bag of money?"
He cried, and darting upon one, he
Shattered his ſkull ſo that it couldn't be trepanned
And ſtretched the robber dead on the ſand.

33. With equally vigorous blows he darted
At t'other robber, who ſtraightway ſtarted,
Finding himself outmatched in fight,
And proceeded to ſeek his ſafety in flight.

34. Hieronimus would, without hesitating,
Have chased the highwayman who was retreating,
But the fellow vanished like the wind,
And left Hieronimus far behind.

35. And now I can scarcely describe the behaviour
Of the gentleman and lady to their saviour,
When, the imminent peril being o'er,
They felt that they could breathe once more.

36. They thanked him, both of them, very sincerely,
And the pretty girl would have kissed him nearly,
If (to say the truth) she had not feared
His unwashed face and his grisly beard.

37. No eulogy can be invented
Which was not by them to him presented,
For the dear Hieronimus, dirty and rough
Was their deliverer, clearly enough.

38. He must go home with them, they insisted,
With a friendliness that could not be resisted,
To their manor-house, where he should be
Richly rewarded for his chivalry.

39. In his present impoverished circumstances
He received with open arms these advances,
And, without further ceremony, thought best
At once to comply with their request.

40. Lifting the coachman they conveyed him
To the carriage in which they laid him,
And, donning the dead highwayman's coat,
Up on the box Hieronimus got.

41. Before, however, Hieronimus mounted,
He found, with a pleaſure not to be recounted,
His bag and almoſt all the money, too,
In the dead highwayman's portmanteau.

42. But the ſtrangeſt thing in all the hiſtory
Was, touching the dead man's face, a myſtery;
There was no longer any plaſter there,
And when Hieronimus scanned it with care,

43. He was not long in taking knowledge
Of a gentleman who, on his journey to college,
Once ſwindled him by hook and by crook,
Herr von Hogier of the great peruke.

44. And ſo this adventure terminated
In a way that our hero greatly elated,
He mounted the coach-box and off he rolled,
Like the knight of the ſorrowful figure of old.

45. And now ere I bring this chapter to a termination,
I inform the readers of the preſent narration,
That this deed is the only honorable one
That Hieronimus has hitherto done.

CHAPTER XXVII.

How Hieronimus was glad to get to Ohnewitz, and how he became ſchoolmaſter there, in a ſchool of little boys and girls.

THAT gentleman and the young lady
Whom Hieronimus reſcued, as mentioned already,
Suſtained the relation of bridegroom and bride
And the knot had been very recently tied.

2. The gentleman had in his jurisdiction
Of caſtles and villages quite a collection,
But the principal one of his private ſeats
Was in the ſmall village of Ohnewitz.

3. To give his lady a gratification
He often made journeys of recreation,
For on very intimate terms he ſtood
With every body in his neighborhood.

4. He had juſt been to viſit a neighboring noble
At the time he met the aforeſaid trouble,
'Twas on his journey home from the ſame,
That the two highwaymen upon him came.

5. They immediately knocked the driver over,
So that they thought he would never recover;
And with violence then demanded next,
His money and other perſonal effects.

6. They alſo from the carriage hauled him,
And would to death have probably mauled him,
When, at the ſhrieks of the agonized dame,
Hieronimus, as we ſaid, to the reſcue came.

7. They related, on the way, this ſtory
To their deliverer, who in his glory
Drove away as merrily now
As the recent terror would allow.

8. Hieronimus likewiſe recounted
How he by the fates had been thus far tormented,
And as, in this way time, quickly flits,
They came, like lightning, to Ohnewitz.

9. Here they ſoon forgot all ſorrow,
And lived without a thought of the morrow,
And made all ſorts of friendly fuſs
In honor to Hieronimus.

10. New clothes, wine, tobacco and coſtly diſhes,
Calculated to gratify the moſt faſtidious wiſhes,
Were furniſhed, enough and ſuperfluous,
At the ſervice of Hieronimus.

11. After ſeveral weeks had been ſpent in this manner,
The gentleman did Hieronimus the honour,
To promiſe that he, for his future ſupport,
Would make proviſion in the very beſt ſort.

12. Now juſt at this time an event tranſpired,
Juſt what Hieronimus would have deſired,
And he ſaw in the coincidence
The hand of a ſpecial Providence.

13. Namely: the Ohnewitz pariſh poſseſses
A ſchool for little maſters and miſses,
Of which the collation unto the lord,
As village patron, the laws did accord.

14. To ſtudy the A, B, C, and the primer,
And learn to read and ſpell, and the grammar,
Theſe branches conſtituted the whole
Of the ſtudies purſued at the aforeſaid ſchool.

15. All opportunities of further learning
The patron removed, with a wiſe diſcerning,
For whenever a peaſant comes to be learned,
At once he grows proud and his brain is turned.

16. Yes, experience teaches us plainly,
That what the peaſant requires mainly
Is to underſtand his almanack, and
To have his catechiſm at his tongue's end.

17. Whenever above this limit he riſes,
His labour he commonly deſpiſes,
And a miſerable confuſion enſues
With the farming proceeds and revenues.

18. Beſides a fixum of thirty dollars, the office
Brought the teacher additional profits
In eggs and butter and turkeys and geeſe
And other perquiſites ſimilar to theſe.

19. And then, at the new year's congratulation,
He went to his lordſhip's houſe to collation,
And alſo received, for attending there,
Of preſents a proportionate ſhare.

20. Now the ſchoolmaſter happened, fortunately,
To have left this world his bleſſing lately,
And the pariſh was thoughtfully looking round
To ſee where a new one might be found.

21. So ſoon as the patron got information
Of this, he tendered the ſituation
To Hieronimus, who ſtraightway
Entered on the office without delay.

22. At firſt, it is true, the life of a teacher
Had not for him one attractive feature,
For he much more account of idleneſs made
Than of ſuch a thankleſs and tedious trade.

23. However, as always, when ſchool was over,
He spent his time at the castle in clover,
Eating and drinking, after awhile
Hieronimus concluded to reconcile

24. Himself to his preſent ſituation,
And attend to its duties with renewed application,
That he might be able to keep the place
All his life till the end of his days.

25. He alſo thought, in many a matter,
To introduce ſome change for the better;
For he found that many faults had crept
Into the ſchool, as heretofore kept.

26. In fact he began, after long deliberation,
To make here and there a reformation,
Which did not, however, turn out very well,
As we to the reader ſhall ſhortly tell.

NOTE.

Heading: *Ohnewitz* means literally *witleſs*.

CHAPTER XXVIII.

How Hieronimus became an Author, and how he edited a new A, B, C,-book, and how he was grievously complained of for it by the Boors to his Lordship.

AT the very firſt entrance on his adminiſtration
Hieronimus found with extremeſt vexation,
That the A, B, C-book hitherto uſed
The minds of the children ſomewhat confuſed.

2. The boys and girls under his ſupervision
Had uſed heretofore the Ballhorn edition,
In which Hieronimus ſoon became aware
Of sundry errors here and there.

3. So, after conſiderable counſel taking
With himſelf, he determined upon making
A ſpeedy new edition of it
Under the following title, to wit:

4. *A new, enlarged and amended edition*
Of the A, B, C-book, under the ſupervision
Of the Author, Hieronimus
Jobs, Theologiæ Candidatus.

5. To the letters with which we're all acquainted,
And which in the alphabet are preſented,
He added alſo the f f t,
Likewiſe the ſch and ſp.

6. The ſpurs of the cock, at the end, who engages
The attention of children of the lower ages,
He omitted with great propriety
From his bran-new book of A, B, C

7. He added, however, for the gratification
Of the juvenile candidates ſor education,
A little neſt with a great egg,
Beſide the ſpurleſs rooſter's leg.

8. This book had ſcarcely entered their presence,
When it was reviewed by the Ohnewitz peaſants,
And the very firſt occaſion gave
For an altercation both fierce and grave.

9. For none of the changes made, whatever,
Found with the critics any favour,
But they every one of them, to a man,
Regarded it as a highly dangerous plan.

10. It could not efcape the obtufeft vifion,
That the author of this new-fangled edition,
Made it exceedingly manifeft,
He was with a paffion for authorfhip poffeffed.

11. As, when, in fultry fummer weather,
Tempeft-brewing vapors mufter together,
Before the crafhing thunder leaps,
A low murmur ordinarily creeps,

12. So here, at firft, in every direction
Was heard a low buzz of difaffection,
And foon the thunderbolt came down
On Hieronimus's crown.

13. The Ohnewitzers by words and dealings
Left him no doubt of the ftate of their feelings,
But he, defying their utmoft rage,
Fell back on his Grace's patronage.

14. The Ohnewitzers would fhow him, however,
That they did not mean to be filent forever:
For every day they did prefer
Some new grievance againft the fchoolmaftér.

15. They therefore, at laft, in town meeting collected,
And the fexton was unanimoufly directed
To draw up a complaint in the following tone:
"High-well-born patron! be it known

16. "*Unto your worſhip by theſe preſents,—*
That we the aſſembled Ohnewitz peaſants
Do take with ſubmiſſion the liberty
To complain of your ſchoolmaſter to thee.

17. "Inasmuch as the ſame has tried our patience
By introducing ſundry innovations,
All under the abſurd pretext
Of remedying exiſting defects.

18. "And has not behaved in the matter, neither,
As a worthy schoolmaſter ſhould, but rather,
Given us peaſants, whom he ought to lead,
A very bad example indeed.

19. "And, only the principal points to mention
Of the grievances to which we would call attention,
Pro primo and in the firſt place, he
Has undertaken arbitrarily

20. "To make a new A, B, C, omitting
The ſpurs of the cock, which is not befitting,
For the ſpurs, aſſuredly, all will agree
An eſſential part of the cock to be.

21. "He alſo diſcourages learning, however,
By making the alphabet longer then ever:
For ſp, ſch, and ſſt
Have ſurely no buſineſs in the A, B, C.

22. "Further, though cocks are never known to
Lay hen's eggs in neſts, as hens are wont to,
Nevertheleſs he has placed one by the cock's leg,
Juſt as if the cock had laid the egg.

23. "Now things like thefe are very bewilderin',
And calculated to miflead the minds of the children,
And a new A, B, C-book, anyhow,
Is an innovation we cannot allow.

24. "*Pro fecundo:* we would not fail to mention
(That the afs's head is an ancient invention,)
Which every child that refifts the rules
Has to wear, as a punifhment, in our fchools.

25. "Now, forely as a fenfitive heart is affected
When to this punifhment it is fubjected,
Still moft of the children make a jeft
Of wearing the afs's head down to their breaft.

26. "Herr Jobs, however, is not contented
With this, but has to the head appended
Neck, body, legs and tail and all
And fo you have now the afs in full.

27. "How the children cry and yell when the teacher
Compels them to wear the entire creature,
And the figure they cut when dreffed up fo,
Can be fcarcely imagined. *Pro tertio:*

28. "Herr Jobs, in addition to the ufual feruling,
Doth barbaroufly box their ears, imperilling
The health of the pupils, and already fome
In confequence have quite deaf become.

29. "*Pro quarto:* the poorer children more than any
Are to be pitied for their cudgellings many,
For, out of respect to perfons, they
Get a double portion every day.

30. "*Pro quinto:* he is in the habit of ſearchin'
The pockets of every ſweet-toothed urchin,
And puts the apples and nuts on the ſhelf,
And after ſchool he eats them himſelf.

31. "*Pro sexto:* his conduct in general ſociety
Is chargeable with much impropriety,
For he leads, they ſay, quite too free a life
With Schulze the boarding-houſe keeper's wife.

32. "He viſits the village tavern daily
And in heated drinks indulges freely,
And many a time has waſted away
Half of the night with Schulze in play.

33. "There are many other complaints, in addition,
Which we would prefer with profound ſubmiſſion;
For very many *gravamina*,
Beſides thoſe already mentioned, there are,

34. "Which at present, however, we forbear ſtating,
Contenting ourſelves with ſupplicating:
That you would be pleaſed, moſt gracious Sir!
To give us another ſchoolmaſtér.

35. "In hope whereof we beg to tarry
Your Grace's ſubjects moſt exemplary.
Given in the village of Ohnewitz.
Etc., etc., etc., etc., etc., etc., etc."

CHAPTER XXIX.

How the diſaffected peaſants of Ohnewitz received a gracious resolution, and how they were adviſed to keep ſilence, and how they were threatened with the dark hole. All in chancery ſtyle.

THE meeting appointed a deputation
Of two to deliver the petition
To his highneſs, the patron; and from the ſame
The following reſolution came:

2. "*We have learned with great diſſatiſfaction,*
From the ſtatement of your recent action,
What grievances you do prefer
Againſt your worthy ſchoolmaſter.

3. "Though, now, it gives us great diſpleaſure
To ſee you reſort to ſuch a meaſure;
We have conſidered, nevertheleſs,
The breadth and length of your grievances.

4. "We cannot, however, up to date diſcover
Anything to make ſuch a fuſs over,
And the proſecution, we decide,
Is altogether unjuſtified.

5. " 'Tis very true, as has been ſaid, he
Has introduced in his ſchool already
A new book of A, B, C, which he
Dedicates to ourſelves ſubmiſſively.

6. " It is alſo clear that, in this edition,
He has made here and there an addition or omiſſion,
It is not however ſo clear to us,
How this can be ſo injurious.

7. " 'Tis true, by an overſight of the engraver,
The cock has loſt his ſpurs; however,
One can very eaſily in the next
Edition remedy ſuch miſtakes.

8. " Our modern reviewers ſeldom take notice
Of ſuch a trifle in books as that is,
But the gentlemen kindly overlook
Such little faults in a new book.

9. " And as regards the interpolations,
They are found in all the early editions;
At leaſt ſch, ſſt, and ſp,
As variations, may be ſuffered to be.

10. " That the cock with an egg ſhould be attended,
Seems indeed leſs capable of being defended,
Yet there's no neceſſity *propter hoc*
To take the egg away from the cock.

11. " For from the egg to draw the concluſion
That the cock had laid it, were great confuſion
In conſcience and reaſon; it proves in fact
No more than the titles to men's names tacked.

12. "And then befides we might have alluded,
To cafes where cockerels over eggs have brooded,
In hoc cafu, undoubtedly,
The cock was a capon properly.

13. "When you propofe as the fecond of the abufes,
That Mr. Jobs a whole afs introduces;
We think therein he commits no offence,
But conducts himfelf as a man of fenfe.

14. "For he means by this no more, nor lefs neither,
Than that you and your children both together,
Old and young and great and fmall,
Are perfect affes incarnate all.

15. "*Pro tertio:* the ear-boxing fo bewilderin',
Which has already made deaf fome children—
We hold it very much amifs
To inflict fuch punifhment as this.

16. "The grievance you have *pro quarto* propounded
We hold to be in fo far well grounded;
For no judge nor fchoolmafter rightfully can
Refpect the perfon of any man.

17. "But for poor no lefs than rich 'tis expedient
That they fhould be punifhed when difobedient,
And punifhment fhould always be
Adminiftered impartially.

18. "When the right of fearch he exercifes,
And fruit in the children's pockets furprifes,
He upholds *pro quinto* the very good rule:
Children fhould not be munching in school!

19. " And as their tender ſtomachs, ſans queſtion,
Find apples and nuts of hard digeſtion,
Here alſo the ſchoolmaſter's plan is good,
To devour, himſelf, ſuch forbidden food.

20. " *Pro sexto*, as to your inſinuation
Touching Schulze's wife's reputation,
Item, the tavern, drinking and dice,
All this in Herr Jobs were a ſhocking vice.

21. "It is our gracious pleaſure, however,
That ſuch things be buried in ſilence forever,
And whoſo ſhall name them again, by my ſoul!
Shall be puniſhed with two days in the hole.

22. "For the reſt, the complaints you have delated
Shall be hereafter more thoroughly inveſtigated,
When from our contemplated tour
We are happily returned once more.

23. "Till then we command you to ceaſe your gabble,
Nor longer in theſe grave matters dabble.
Given at our reſidence etc., etc."
"Reſolution for the Peaſants of Ohnewitz."

CHAPTER XXX.

How, one Wednesday, a riot broke out at Ohnewitz, and all sorts of signs and wonders preceded it, and how Herr Hieronimus was driven away with cudgels, &c.

IT may well be conceived that this resolution
Threw the whole village into the greatest confusion,
In fact there arose on all sides a hum
Among the peasants, both mighty and grum.

2. For now it was clearly manifested
That Jobs was by the patron assisted,
And that justice could no longer have course,
And they swore to avenge themselves by force.

3. In this weighty crisis they often came together
To consult in the tavern with one another,
And with beer and tobacco considered there
How they could best approach the affair.

4. They first determined, with a sweeping
Unanimity, on keeping
Their children at home, and not one of all
In fact went to school again, great or small.

5. But the wiſeſt of them adviſed, with reaſon,
To lie in wait for a favorable ſeaſon,
For then, when came the fitting hour,
They could all ariſe at once in their power.

6. They all gave in at once their adheſion
To ſuch a ſenſible propoſition,
And ſo they fixed upon a day
When the patron ſhould happen to be away.

7. 'Tis true theſe arrangements were all to lie ſleeping,
In every boſom's ſecret keeping
Till the terrible moon ſhould be uſhered in
When the diſturbance was to begin.

8. But before theſe great events had being,
Signs and wonders had men been ſeeing,
As on the eve of important events
Men commonly witneſs premonitory porténts.

9. For example, a ſhort time before, at the hour
Of midnight, a very great owl on the tower
Of the church had been heard to utter a cry
Frightful and loud to the inky ſky.

10. Likewiſe had one of the Ohnewitz people
Coming from the inn, heard a tolling in the ſteeple;
Alſo the very old chimney fell down
On the ſchool-houſe roof with an awful ſound.

11. Likewiſe the ſexton's cow give birth to
The longeſt eared calf perhaps on earth too;
Likewiſe many dogs ran howling round
Through the village with a horrible ſound.

12. Ignes fatui were ſeen in many places,
And ſometimes by night ſtrange forms and faces;
Likewiſe at noonday it came to paſs,
A leg was broke of the miller's aſs.

13. All this appeared the prefiguration
Of ſome impending revelation;
But no one noticed the danger until
The prophecies did themſelves fulfil.

14. Now it was exactly on Wedneſday morning,
That the riot broke out without any warning,
When, at eight preciſely, every boor
Was ſeen to iſſue from his door.

15. It was dreadful to think on what might happen,
For every one was armed with a weapon,
And forth the confederates all ſwarmed,
With clubs and flails in great numbers armed.

16. All was now aſtir in the village,
One would have propheſied murder and pillage,
And every dog and rooſter now
Began at once to bark and crow.

17. On the village common ſoon collected
The mighty maſs of the diſaffected,
And in proceſſion proceeded thence
Straight to the ſchoolmaſter's reſidence.

18. Many children came thronging after
On both ſides, full of joy and laughter,
To think that they would be free to-day
And the bad ſchoolmaſter ſent away.

19. Herr Jobs in his bed was lying quiet,
Never once dreaming of any riot,
When all on a ſudden the whole ſwarm
Broke in upon him with a great alarm.

20. He opened his eyes in conſternation,
And vehement was his agitation,
As now for the firſt time he did mark
The treaſon that had been brewing in the dark.

21. They fell upon him with precipitation,
Leaving him ſmall time for heſitation;
Only, in conſideration of the preſent diſtreſs,
They gave him leave to put on his dreſs:

22. Then advifed him to leave Ohnewitz behind him,
And never again let one of them find him;
They added likewife many a fcoff,
And cudgelled and pelted our hero off.

23. And fo this action was completed
And the expedition fuccefsfully treated,
And with a loud ju! hu! ju! hu!
All to the tavern now withdrew.

24. And every one fwore with a terrible clatter,
That he had done the beft in the matter,
And in drinking brandy determined that he
The greateft hero of all would be.

25. There were fome, however, had no fatisfaction,
But only remorfe for the whole tranfaction,
And they fully expected to find their reward
In the dark hole, at the return of their lord.

Note.

Stanza 9. So in Virgil (Aen. IV. 462,) among the portents that preceded the death of Dido:

"*Solaque culminibus ferali carmine bubo*
Sæpe queri, et longas in fletum ducere voces."

—"With a boding note
The folitary fcreech-owl ftrains her throat,
And on a chimney's top or turret's height,
With fongs obfcene difturbs the filence of the night."—

Dryden.

CHAPTER XXXI.

How Hieronimus in his flight to Bavaria and a new adventure, in meeting his beloved Amelia on the ſtage at the theatre. Very pleaſant to read.

AS the fox, when he leaves the hounds behind him
And flies where they no more can find him,
Is glad that only a mouthful of hair
He has had to loſe, which he well could ſpare,—

2. So Hieronimus, in his greateſt tribulation,
Took to himſelf the ſame conſolation,
And was very glad, upon his ſoul,
To have 'ſcaped the boors with a ſkin whole.

3. 'Tis true he had learned, in his ſudden departure
From Ohnewitz, ſomething he had to ſmart for,
How very sour and bitter and hard
Was a poor ſchoolmaſter's reward.

4. He alſo made a vow that he never
Would publiſh again any books whatever,
For his flogging and flight, he had to own,
Were owing to the authorſhip-mania alone.

5. Meanwhile as his patron (we've ſtated already,)
Was gone on a tour to Bavaria with his lady;
Hieronimus determined to go there to him,
For refuge from the wrath of the peaſants ſo grim.

6. The journey took no great time to plan it,
In fact he no ſooner reſolved than began it;
But ſoon, before he was far on his way,
A new adventure cauſed his delay.

7. For contrary to all expectation
His plans met a ſudden pertubation,
Soon after he reached a great city, where
He intended to reſt a day or two there.

8. Here, to conſole and divert himſelf ſolely
And drive away care and melancholy,
It came into his head one day,
That he that evening would go to the play.

9. He ſoon perceived among the actreſſes,
Of beautiful faces and ſplendid dreſſes,
One who in face, voice, form and hair,
Was the image of his Amelia fair.

10. Heavens! what rapture his heart did fire,
That he ſhould ſo unexpectedly ſpy her!
The entire pit was almoſt thrown
Into confuſion by this fact alone.

11. And hardly had ſhe her performance ended,
When into the green-room he inſtantly bounded,
And now there was many a joyful buſs
'Twixt her and her dear Hieronimus.

12. Both were curious to hear from each other,
What ſingular fortune thus brought them together;
 Hieronimus therefore was glad enough,
 With her to ſnug quarters to hurry off.

13. Then and there did Amelia get her firſt information
Of the wonders ſet down in the previous narration,
 As having tranſpired ſince the memorable night,
 When the old gent drove him forth in ſuch plight.

14. And of his adventures with the ſpiritual lady,
And the diſhonorable attempt ſhe made, he
 Told, and how, ſubſequently, the whole
 Of his money by night in a tavern was ſtole.

15. And how, in the wood he deſpatched a villain,
And reſcued a nobleman whom he was killin',
 And became by one of his lucky hits,
 A ſchoolmaſter at Ohnewitz.

16. And his ſubſequent trials and tribulation,
And how he now againſt all expectation,
 Had found her in the theatre here,
 All this he copiouſly poured in her ear.

17. Hieronimus, now, in his turn, deſired
To hear what in her experience had tranſpired,
 And the fair one proceeded to relate,
 As follows, her hiſtory up to date.

CHAPTER XXXII.

How the damſel Amelia tells Hieronimus the ſtory of her life. A very long chapter, becauſe the perſon ſpeaking is a female. Exactly one hundred verſes.

"AMELIA Ripraps my proper name is:
The place where into the world I came, is
The celebrated town of A. A.
There I firſt ſaw the light of day.

2. "My father was an advocate, had many cases
Both there and in the neighboring places,
For he knew the *jura* thoroughly
And understood chicanery.

3. "The most complicated cases he would take'em
And still more complicated make'em,
And many an art and trick he knew
For spinning out short cases, too.

4. "His ingenuity many a clever
Rogue from the gallows did deliver;
And, by recommending the crime
Of perjury just in the nick of time,

5. "He brought off many a cheat inglorious,
Over his honorable opponent victorious,
Relieved many a one of sore distress
And many a poor devil of his bread, I guess.

6. "He hated peace and compromising,
Much rather, in every case, advising,
However trifling the matter might be,
Recourse to law and chicanery.

7. "He kept his clients in a round of dances
Through all possible legal *instánces*,
And kept them appealing, on and on,
Until their very last penny was gone.

8. "For the rest, he served to the best of his science
And fidelity the clients who placed on him reliance,
Yet, now and then, for variety's sake,
From the opposite party a bribe would take.

9. "Of a tolerable property he thus got poſſeſſion;
What to others was a curſe, was to him a bleſſing,
And when to wrangling and quarrelling fell,
He took the oyſter and gave each a ſhell.

10. "My bleſſed mother was the daughter
Of a wealthy farmer of the higheſt order,
Who litigated to ſuch a degree
That he ruined himſelf and his property.

11. "My father had ſerved him as advocate duly
And given him counſel faithfully and truly,
And ſo at length, he got for his pay
The farmer's pretty daughter one day.

12. "She had already rejected many
Who offered their hands in matrimony,
At the time when her father was yet well off
And had property enough.

13. "But as the incomes began to grow fewer,
No one cared any longer to woo her;
For the pretty pennileſs face that goes
Will never tempt the men to propoſe.

14. "She managed after awhile, however,
To catch my father, for ſhe was clever,
And grounded to the laſt degree
In all the arts of gallantry.

15. "My father took a fancy to her,
And ſo, as aforeſaid, became her wooer,
And, wiſhing a partner of his life,
Beſought her of the farmer for wife.

16. "They tasted together many enjoyments
In their wedded life, and little annoyance,
At least for the first three months or so,
While marriage was yet a new thing, you know.

17. "And then her fine face and agreeable manner
Many a private income won her,
When some rich party happened to be
Attentive to her particularly.

18. They managed to get from parties in cases
A matter or two for household uses;
For the advocate's lady always got
What the advocate, her Lord, did not.

19. "When her husband to his pleadings attended,
She meanwhile was not idle-handed,
And at such times in her apartments she
Had private hearings generally.

20. "Now though I cannot positively declare it
For a fact, and solemnly swear it,
That the above named advocate
Was my real father—at any rate

21. "I never in my life have heard the suggestion
That he so much as raised a question,
When, after about a year, may be,
My mother was delivered of me.

22. "The earlier parts of my childish history
Remain involved in the shades of mystery,
However my father and mother loved me
As their only daughter tenderly.

23. "No pains were ſpared on the formation
Of my manners and my education,
And they ſent me to ſchool at an early age
In the uſual ſtudies there to engage.

24. "They ſtrictly forbade, however, the teachers
To inflict on me blows or bitter ſpeeches,
And in everything, ſmall as it might be,
My will was conſulted carefully.

25. "When I ſcarcely was ten years old, my fancies
Began to devour all ſorts of romances,
And already far more of love I knew
Than other maidens of eighteen do.

26. "I was happy and vain to receive addreſſes
From pretty young men, and ſometimes careſſes,
And many a practical romance
In my thirteenth year did already commence.

27. "Perhaps 'twas a fault of my education,
That I felt very early an inclination,
Which never has yet my nature left,—
A ſecret inclination to theft.

28. "My parents, ſmitten with fatal blindneſs,
Called it childiſh ſport in their miſplaced kindneſs,
And when I was caught in ſome wicked craft,
At their ſly little daughter they only laughed.

29. "My fifteenth year was hardly over,
When I had already many a lover,
Which, with one of my not ugly face,
Could hardly fail of being the caſe.

30. "Some of them ſeemed quite preſentable
In my father's eyes, at leaſt not contemptible;
My mother, however, found in the ſame
Many a thing to diſlike and blame.

31. "It muſt be a man of high poſition,
Equal to any in the land in condition,
Such a one or none, ſhe ſaid,
Who ſhould ever her pretty daughter wed.

32. "But no man came, of high condition,
With a matrimonial propoſition,
And to me it began to be tireſome
Waiting for ſuitors who didn't come.

33. "I therefore thought in ſome other manner
To ſave from tarniſh my pride and honour,
And to meet the handſome young men I flew
To many a ſecret rendez-vous.

34. "Fearing there might be ſome miſcarriage,
Which would perhaps to my future marriage
Prove an obſtacle, if ſhe
Allowed me too much liberty,

35. "My mother took it in contemplation
To lay on my love-tricks ſome limitation,
And by day and by night henceforward took
Notes of my every ſtep and look.

36. "Now though its indulgence was thus prevented
The paſſion itſelf was rather augmented,
For a ſtrictly forbidden fruit will be
Sought always the more eagerly.

37. "And the greater the hindrance the more the desire,
So did it with my inclination transpire,
For I sought every opportunity
To gratify it secretly.

38. "By night through my window often glided
Ghosts with flesh and bones provided,
Which then would usually half the night
Stay with me till morning light.

39. "And when I happened to find nothing better
I got now and then a love-letter
Of such heart-breaking tenor, as we
Daily in every romance may see.

40. "My nineteenth year had exactly ended
When I one evening a ball attended,
And there with a gentleman acquainted became
Herr Baron Von Hogier was his name."

41. Hieronimus here interrupted her talking;
"Herr Von Hogier? the thing is shocking!
His name, as well as his rank, the whole
Is familiar enough to me, by my soul!

42. "Herr Von Hogier was a sharper, I tell ye!"
"He was *all of that,*" resumed Amelia,
"And, dear Hieronimus, you shall see
What took place between him and me.

43. "To Herr Von Hogier I took a great liking,
His person and manners were very striking,
His elegant dress and great peruke
At the very first moment my fancy took.

44. "He made me a very flattering propoſal
Placed his hand and fortune at my diſpoſal,
  And what pleaſed and flattered me far more,
  I was his only angel, he ſwore.

45. "He alſo ſaid much of his goods and poſſeſſions
Situated in the land of the Heſſians,
  Though he now was travelling to and fro
  Through the world incognito.

46. "He did alſo diſtinctly inſtruct me
He'd like, if I pleaſed, from home to abduct me,
  If I at the hour appointed would ſtand
  Ready, with money and jewels in hand.

47. "And ſo, by night, when nothing hindered,
The coffers and cheſts at home I plundered,
  Pocketed what I found without fear
  And took my flight with Herr Von Hogier.

48. "We made our retreat in very good order,
'Till we about reached the laſt Swabian border;
  And during the firſt four days of our ride,
  Did not reſt twelve hours, I'm ſatisfied.

49. "What my parents thought, and how aſtounded,
To find bags empty and daughter abſconded,
  And how they took on and ſwore and ſtormed,
  You may well imagine but cannot be informed.

50. "When we at laſt arrived at W,
(Not with too long a ſtory to trouble you)
  We determined to tarry ſome days there
  To reſt ourſelves and get good fare.

51. "We, therefore, as we proposed to, tarried,
And lived as cosy as if we were married,
And the Herr Baron Von Hogier
Behaved very tenderly to his dear.

52. "I therefore was now, in my own opinion,
Happier than a Queen in her dominion,
And thought of nothing but joy and glee
And pleasure and festivity.

53. "But close on my heels was misfortune pursuing,
For before I could dream of anything brewing,
Suddenly and secretly one night
Herr Von Hogier, *per post*, took flight.

54. "My money, too, dear Hieronimus, (think on't,)
And my jewels were gone to the dogs in an instant,
And of the valuables the whole
Which I from my parents before had stole.

55. "I saw now, with all his cooing and billin',
That Herr Von Hogier was a settled villain,
And that matters did not rightly stand
With his estate in the Hessian land.

56. "You can therefore easily imagine
How much I took this thing in dudgeon,
For I had not dreamed that the Herr Von Hogier
Could be guilty of such tricks as this 'ere.

57. "Now left alone and by all forsaken,
I knew not what step was next to be taken,
And in desperation I looked around
To see where a refuge could be found.

58. "That I ſhould go back again to my parents
Was an impoſſible occurrence,
For ſuch a courſe would certainly
Have been very uncomfortable to me.

59. "However I ſtill, as a ſlight conſolation,
Had twenty-four ducats remaining in my poſſeſſion,
Which I, in caſe of future diſtreſs,
Had ſewed into my under-dreſs.

60. "Theſe twenty-four ducats, I now bethought me,
A ſpecial fortune ſeems to have brought me,
For they are now, moſt certainly,
All my eſtate and property.

61. "I would not any longer tarry
But after Herr Von Hogier hurry,
And on the very ſelf-ſame day,
I took the ſtage and drove away.

62. "For I had at the poſt-houſe received information
That he hired an extra for the occaſion,
And was therefore probably by this,
In Swabia, as one might gueſs.

63. "If at that time I could have caught him,
To juſtice I at once would have brought him,
And I ſhould certainly have then
Got all my money back again.

64. "It was, my dear, in this occupation,
That on the well remembered occaſion,
I found in the ſtage coach a ſad young man,
With whom my acquaintance then firſt began.

65. "For the reſt, up to this time I have never
Succeeded in getting any glimpſe whatever,
Nor have ſo much as been able to hear
Of the whereabouts of Herr Von Hogier."

66. Here Hieronimus could not help breaking
In once again on Amelia ſpeaking:
"Potz tauſend! I know well," he ſaid,
Where Herr Von Hogier the ſcamp has fled.

67. "Shortly before our acquaintance, dear Amelia!
Herr Von Hogier, the son of Belial,
Spunged me out of much money one day
At a tavern by his tricky play.

68. "This was the principal occaſion
Of my melancholy ſituation
Of mind, which I at laſt forgot
When in the ſtage by your ſide I ſot.

69. "Herr Von Hogier, too, was one of the couple
Of travellers, diſguiſed as merchant people,
Who after ſupper at the inn
Stole my money bag and all therein.

70. "The robber too, whom I killed, (as already
Stated,) when I ſaved the gentleman and lady,
Was verily, by his perſon and face,
No other than this ſame ſcape-grace.

71. "You, therefore, now may reſt contented:
His future villanies are prevented,
And I have thus moſt righteouſly
Avenged myſelf for his knavery."

72. Amelia replied: "Thy histories,
My dear! are full of curious myſteries,
And ſo remarkable each event,
It fills me with aſtoniſhment!

73. "The proverb: *what is ſpun however finely,*
Is ſure to come to the ſunlight finally,
Turns out exactly to a hair
In the case of that raſcal Hogier there.

74. "But to proceed in my own narration,
At the time of our ſudden ſeparation,
On account of the watch I concluded to go on,
A while, on foot, and all alone.

75. "About that time, by good luek's providing,
An elderly gentleman came riding
Along in his carriage, and when he ſpied
Me trudging on by the roadſide,

76. "With ſuch a ſignificant ſmile he beckoned,
That I was ſitting by him in a ſecond;
And, as my perſon pleaſed him, he
Made a propoſition to me:

77. "To be his chambermaid, and aid him
Drive off the blues that did often invade him,
For he lived alone without any wife,
And was an old bachelor for life.

78. "Now it would have been dangerous, I concluded,
And certainly I ſhould be deluded,
(So the thing began now to appear,)
To ſeek any further for Herr Von Hogier.

79. "And ſo I could not make refuſal
To the old gentleman's kind propoſal,
Although his age and his gray hair,
Were not juſt ſuch as I wiſhed they were.

80. "So I took up with him my habitation
And gave him effectual conſolation,
And I behaved myſelf to him
As if I his lawful ſpouſe had been.

81. "He thereſore held me in high eſtimation,
And gave me the whole houſe-adminiſtration,
And all the ſervants, maids and men,
Subjected to my regimen.

82. "I superintended cellars and preſſes,
Kitchen and chamber and wardrobe and dreſſes,
Saw to the waſhing, table and bed,
And everything that came under that head.

83. "The keys of the cheſts, the plates and platters,
And even the more valuable matters,
The linen and ſilver, were to me
Committed into cuſtody.

84. "And from many an evening till the morrow,
I beguiled the old gentleman of his ſorrow,
And gave his troubled ſpirit eaſe
And miniſtered to his neceſſities.

85. "For the old gentleman would never
Do the leaſt thing without me whatever,
And nothing in any departmént,
Could ever take place without my consent.

86. "Of courſe, in addition to my compenſation,
I received from him many a valuable donation,
And, to make up any deficiency,
I ſtole a trifle occaſionally.

87. "Although now nothing external was wanting,
There was ſomething always my ſpirit haunting,
And the time ſeemed long when I began
To live with the old gentleman.

88. "'Tis true in the courſe of time the houſe-writer
Did make my ſpirits a little lighter,
But, being rather ſickly, he
Was not very intereſting to me.

89. "I found it for my comfort neceſſary,
After his death to get a new ſecretary,
And you, my dear, juſt then applied
For the vacant place of the one who had died.

90. "I had for you a prepoſeſſion,
At the very firſt ſight, I muſt make the confeſſion;
And this, you ſee, was the reaſon why
I ſpoke in your favour ſo earneſtly.

91. "Of all the things that between us tranſpired,
From the time that you were firſt hired
'Till the night he found you in my room,
Dear Hieronimus! you are aware, I preſume.

92. "When he at that time diſmiſſed you,
I need not ſay how much I miſſed you,
But the old man continued all the more
To give ſharp hints on that very ſcore.

93. "His anger did my ſpirits gall ſo,
That I came very near leaving alſo,
And it was about as much as I could do
With my careſſes to bring him to.

94. "Meanwhile, from that time, his inclination
For me gave place to alienation,
And to a new young kitchen maid
All his attention henceforth he paid.

95. "And therefore to relieve the depreſſion
Of ſpirits your abſence did occaſion,
I lived thenceforward ſomewhat free
With the old gentleman's lackéy.

96. "But when our intercourſe he did diſcover,
All chance of reconciliation was over,
No word of excuſe would he wait to hear—
I muſt pack up my duds at once and clear.

97. "Being now with money tolerably provided,
To travel through the world I decided,
'Till ſome new opportunity
Of future ſupport ſhould turn up for me.

98. "While through this neighborhood I wandered
A band of players I encountered,
And at my requeſt the company
For a new actreſs accepted me.

99. "Already ſome months have I been ſtaying
With them and in their ſervice playing
Exceedingly well, as I'm inclined
To think, the parts to me aſſigned.

100. "For the rest, it gratifies me greatly
To think of the good luck that lately
Has brought together you and me
For the third time so happily."

CHAPTER XXXIII.

How Hieronimus conceived a desire to be a play-actor, and how he was persuaded thereto by Miss Amelia.

HIERONIMUS exceedingly wondered
At the story told in the previous hundred
Verses, and quite forgot, from this day,
His patron and Bavaria.

2. He now determined that he never
Would leave Amelia on any account whatever,
And consequently took it in view
That he would be a comedian too.

3. When Amelia got information
Of this, she approved his determination,
And extolled her profession's dignity
In the following apology:

4. "I know from many an example,
That the stage-player's profession has ample
Claim to be called the worthiest
Of all that in the world exist.

5. "For the theatre holds up a mirror
In which one sees, even plainer and clearer
Than in the world itself, how odd
Is the mixture in life of good and bad.

6. "Now we have merry comedies,
And now we have tearful tragedies;
Now they laugh and dance and ſing,
And now ſigh and groan and all that ſort of thing.

7. "Now comical farces excite our laughter,
Now tears and bloodſhed follow right after;
Now one is poor and now he's rich:
To-day in the parlor, the next in the ditch.

8. "Now he's a peaſant and now he's a ruler,
Now he's a fool and now he's a ſcholar;
Now he is young and now he is old,
Now he is warm and now he is cold.

9. "Now he is ſober, now he is tipſy,
Now he's a capuchin, now he's a gipſy;
Now he's a beggar and now he's a baron,
Now he's a varlet and now a Herr Von.

10. "Now a renowniſt and now a lackey,
Now a chamberlain and now a blackey;
Now a landlord and now a gueſt,
Now a cowherd and now a prieſt.

11. "Now a paſtor—a philoſopher famous,
Now a ſexton—an ignoramus;
Now a monarch and now a fudge,
Now a hangman and now a judge.

12. "Through theſe and other ſimilar changes,
One, ever newly delighted, ranges,
And the courſe of the world is faithfully
Repreſented in all its variety.

13. "If we only play with all our powers
The parts which for the time are ours,
The audience applaud at the end
With a vehement clapping of the hand.

14. "On the contrary, when we fail or blunder,
The audience is down on us like thunder
The pit and galleries all laugh,
And hiſs and yell and hoot us off."

15. "Your account, dear Amelia, I cannot deny it,
Pleaſes me ſo, I'm diſpoſed to try it,"
Anſwered with a hearty buſs
The new play-actor Hieronimus.

16. He was now to the manager preſented
And to him by Amelia recommended,
And on the next day following he
Was enrolled in the acting company.

CHAPTER XXXIV.

How Hieronimus became a real player, and how Miſs Amelia was falſe to him and ran off with a rich gentleman, and how he alſo in deſperation went away.

INDULGENT reader! thou ſhalt now be inſtructed
How in his new profeſſion Hieronimus conducted,
When once the manager had tried
His qualifications, and was ſatisfied.

2. Drunken ſtudents and profligate preachers,
Laughable ſextons and ſtupid teachers,
Secretaries amorouſly inclined,
Poltroons and rakes, and parts of that kind.

3. All theſe Hieronimus played to perfection,
Becauſe for ſuch he'd a natural predilection,
And every time he appeared therein,
A general round of applauſe did win.

4. And when an author he did enact, or
Appeared in a ſchoolmaſter's character,
Now and then one ſeemed to ſee
The author or ſchoolmaſter bodily.

5. But when the philofopher's part he affected,
No great applaufe could be expected,
And in fentimental paftoral
Hieronimus was juft next to nothing at all.

6. He played the fine gentleman very badly,
And, as a general thing, failed fadly
In any thing like a refpectable part,
Or where there was much to be got by heart.

7. Hieronimus in this new employment
Experienced unalloyed enjoyment,
And blifsfully flew the moments away
In the arms of his queen—his Amelia.

8. He would not in his love-intoxication
Have exchanged for a king's his fituation,
And all his trouble and forrow, at laft,
Seemed to be over and ended and paft.

9. But how very feldom one of us liftens
To the proverb "All is not gold that gliftens."
Fortune often takes a freak
And plays us an unexpected trick.

10. Hieronimus (as you'll fee by what fhall follow)
Was fated to find her promifes hollow,
For when he leaft dreamed of fuch a thing,
The greateft joy of his life took wing

11. The forrow by which he was now o'ertaken
The heavieft of all he did reckon,
Namely, his moft dearly beloved
Amelia unfaithful proved.

12. It happened thus: on a certain occasion
A rich young gentleman of consideration,
Saw the enchanting Amelia
Perform at the theatre in a play.

13. Now as there are ninnies all the world over,
He immediately became her lover,
And Amelia was shrewd enough
Not to treat him with a rebuff.

14. In reading her history we easily discover
That she had a great inclination, moreover,
(Because she was a woman, you see)
To frequent change and variety.

15. The rich young man frequent visits paid her,
For which Hieronimus did upbraid her,
His face grew black and his eyes grew red,
And in his despair he wished himself dead.

16. But that only made him less amiable
To Amelia, and daily more intolerable,
And very soon he received from her
A renunciation *formaliter*.

17. When this blight fell on his affections,
He at once dissolved his theatrical connexions,
And in extreme desperation of mind
Left the scene of disgrace behind.

18. That we here may bring the narration
Of Amelia's life to a termination,
She left with the gentleman, and it is said,
Died two years after in child-bed.

CHAPTER XXXV.

How Hieronimus returned home to Schildburg, and how he found there all ſorts of changes.

AND ſo Hieronimus was fated
To wander again, as above narrated,
And never before in his life had he
Set out ſo diſcontentedly.

2. Amelia's unlooked for infidelity
Seemed every hour a new reality,
And in his deſpair he could ſcarcely keep
Himſelf from taking the fatal leap.

3. 'Tis true, if I may expreſs an opinion,
His patron in the Bavarian dominion
Would have been, in his preſent afflicted ſtate,
His ſureſt refuge from adverſe fate.

4. But one who falls into tribulation
Is apt to loſe his ſelf-poſſeſſion,
And at ſuch times, ('tis the general rule,)
Reſigns his wits and acts the fool.

5. And ſo in utter deſperation
Hieronimus formed the determination
That he would now his ſteps retrace
To Schildeburg, his native place.

6. And now as he met with no detention
On his journey homeward, worthy of mention,
He did at laſt, thank Heaven! arrive
At the place of his deſtination, alive.

7. Here, when the firſt ſalutations were over,
He very ſoon began to diſcover
That many changes had taken place
In his long abſence from the place.

8. His mother, indeed, he found ſtill living,
But in outward circumſtances far from thriving,
Indeed her means were very ſtrait,
And her bread was earned with trouble great.

9. He learned with ſorrow, that one brother
Had gone the way of all fleſh, another
Had opened a little Nuremberg ſhop,
Whereby he managed to fill his crop.

10. The eldeſt brother had ſucceſsfully courted
The uglieſt woman the country ſupported,
But the money which ſhe did poſſeſs
Made him forget her uglineſs.

11. He alſo learned that his eldeſt ſiſter
Had connected herſelf in marriage with Miſter
Kircher, the ſexton of the place,
And lived with him in pretty good caſe.

12. His ſiſter Gertrude one Mr. Geier
Had wedded, and become a father by her,
But thereupon was off like the wind,
And left both bride and infant behind.

13. She tried her beſt to earn her living,
Her ſervices indiſcriminately giving
To young people of the richer ſort,
From whom ſhe thus received a ſupport.

14. Another ſiſter, they did inform him,
An old widower took to keep houſe and warm him,
And, in ſo far, appeared to be
Living with him in peace and unity.

15. And, laſt of all, his younger ſiſter,
A blooming maiden, whoſe name was Eſther,
Did ſtill to her mother ſolace afford,
And get from her her daily board.

16. Now, Hieronimus's return made his mother
Very happy, and no doubt, each ſiſter and brother,
Becauſe they ſo long had not ſeen him, nor heard
Of his whereabouts a ſingle word:

17. Still, at the ſame time, it would not do for
Him to be living at home as a loafer,
And ſo they began to take in view
What buſineſs there was Hieronimus might do.

CHAPTER XXXVI.

How Hieronimus became a night-watchman in Schildburg, and how his mother's dream and Mrs. Urgalindina's prophecy were fulfilled.

NOW it came to paſs that the man they hired
As watchman in Schildburg had lately expired,
And ſo the office was lying void,
Vacant, empty and unſupplied.

2. As, now, in all ftates that are ordered rightly,
The watchman can't be difpenfed with nightly;
The burghers confulted in the prefent cafe
On ordaining another to fill his place.

3. Now many fit fubjects might have been felected
Who to taking the office would not have objected,
But, on account of his powerful voice,
Hieronimus feemed to be their choice.

4. 'Tis true fome perfons at firft made objections
And caft upon him perfonal reflections,
As if Hieronimus would not do
Exactly for the office in view.

5. For the city would not, fo they contended,
If he were watchman, be well defended,
For how could he who preferred to fleep
When he ought to wake, the city keep?

6. Neverthelefs did Hieronimus
Very foon receive a unanimous
Invitation from the *bourgeoifie*
That he would the new night-watchman be.

7. But firft it would be neceffary
His predeceffor's widow he fhould marry,
For the deceafed had ftood very high
In the city's efteem defervedly.

8. And fo, by way of compenfation
To his highly afflicted widow, the corporation
To the other qualifications tacked on
The marrying of her perfon as a *fine qua non*.

9. Now, as her age was thirty only,
And her perſon certainly not very homely,
Hieronimus accepted the terms propoſed
And his predeceſſor's widow eſpouſed.

10. And now to old and young, as they ſlumbered,
The hours of night were again muſically numbered,
For Hieronimus, the new
Watchman put his horn to his mouth and blew.

11. And whenever the clock was heard from the tower,
He began as follows to call the hour:
"Hark ye, gentlemen, as ye lie there ſtill,
And hear what I to you ſing and tell:

12. "The clock has juſt proclaimed the hour,
Twelve, one, two, three, from the old church tower;
Take care, if I may you adviſe,
Of fire and light and your daughters likewiſe!

13. "That no one may ſet anything on fire,
Or any other harm may tranſpire,
Be careful, thereſore, and ſee to 't,
To 't, to 't, to 't, toot! toot! toot! toot!"

14. For the reſt he ſteadily conducted
Himſelf as a watchman well inſtructed;
Slept ſoundly all day long that he
Might at night more wakeful be.

15. In all the time of his ſinging and watching
No thief dared riſk his power of catching,
So that Schildburg was entirely free
From all nocturnal burglary.

16. And every citizen, however foundly fnoring,
Woke when Hieronimus his blaft was pouring,
And the found of his horn and his nightly call
Were heard throughout the town by all.

17. A wonderful coincidence this muft be reekoned
With Frau Jobs's dream (in chapter fecond,)
And all turns out, to a hair, for us
In the cafe of the watch Hieronimus.

18. And that which Urgalindina ftated,
When about the boy's future interrogated,
On the ground of chiromantic art,
Was verified now in every part.

19. Now that the things were fulfilled completely,
The explanation could be made very neatly,
As with prophecies is always the cafe;
They're myfteries till the event takes place.

20. Meantime Frau Schnepperle's talk (remember)
When Frau Jobs was keeping child-chamber,
(As may be read in chapter 3)
Has not as yet been fulfilled, you fee.

21. And, from our prefent information,
We fhould fay that Frau Schnepperle's reputation
In the matter of phyfiognomy
Muft fuffer very confiderably.

CHAPTER XXXVII.

How Hieronimus received a viſit from friend Death, who took him to his reſt. A chapter which would do for a funeral ſermon.

THERE'S a ſenſible ſaying which, for ages,
As is very well known to all of us ſages,
Through learned books has run its round,
(In the old church-father Horace 'tis found :)

2. *As well against the palace portals,*
As against the doors of the poorest mortals,
Friend Death, who is everywhere well-known,
Knocks with his old dry knuckle-bone.

3. That is, when popularly translated,
All that lives to die is fated,
As well the monarch as the boor,
As well the rich man as the poor.

4. Inasmuch as friend Death makes not the smallest
Distinction between the lowest and tallest,
But cuts down all both low and high,
With the strictest impartiality.

5. And, as he ever slyly watches,
The cavalier and the clown he catches,
The beggar and also the great Sultán,
The tailor and also the Tartar Khan.

6. And with his scythe his rounds he goeth
And honorables and lackeys moweth,
The herdsmaid and the titled dame,
Without distinction of place or name.

7. He listens to no compromises;
Both crowns and bag-wigs he despises,
Doctor's hats and stag's horns
And whatever else men's heads adorns.

8. A thousand things he has command of,
By which he us can make an end of,
And now the dagger, and now the pest,
And now a grape-stone, gives us rest.

9. A ſickneſs now and now a panic,
And now a miſtaken doſe of arſénic,
Poiſon or pleaſure or very ſpite,
Or love or grief or a mad dog's bite.

10. Now a law-ſuit and now a ſplinter,
Now a bad woman and now a bad winter,
Now a nooſe or other ſnare,
Of which may Heaven help us beware.

11. Againſt his darts, when they aſſail us,
No d'Arçon's floating batteries 'll avail us,
Friend Death, the ravenous, is not ſcared
By cannon or fortreſs, ſhield or ſword.

12. The commandant of the Seven Towers,
The grand vizier in his harem's bowers,
As well as Diogenes in his tub,
All—all are ſwallowed by him for grub.

13. So is it as far as memory reaches,
As far as ancient hiſtory teaches;
Jacob Böhme and Ariſtotlés,
Klaus Narre and Demoſthenes;

14. Misſhapen Eſop his fables tellin',
And the Grecian beauty, world-famed Helen,
Unhappy Job and King Solomon,
Gave up the ghoſt and now are gone.

15. Emperor Max and Jobs the Senátor
Virgil and Hans Sachs my ancéſtor,
Goliath great and David ſmall,
Early or late, they periſhed all.

16. Nicholas Klimm and Marcus Aurelius,
Cato and Eulenſpiegelius,
Ritter Samſon and old Don
Quixote, alas, they are dead and gone.

17. Kartouche and King Alexander together,
As like each other as birds of a feather,
Bramarbas the hero and Hannibal,
Met the common deſtiny all.

18. Great Auguſtus, alſo Poland's
Hero and Charles XII., nolens volens,
As well as the Perſian Shah Kulikan
And Czar Peter, that famous man;

19. Item, Xerxes, with his hoſt ſo enormous,
Potiphar, of whom the ſcriptures inform us,
And Polyphemus, the one-eyed,
And old Methuſalem have died.

20. All—all—to the grave they had to carry,
Calvin and Father Santa Clara,
Likewiſe the Patriach Abraham
And alſo Eraſmus of Rotterdam.

21. Müller Arnold, too, and the Ruſſian
Imperial Dynaſty and the Pruſſian
Lawyers, and April, well known,
Who fell down ſtairs at Ratiſbon.

22. All—all—have ſunk beneath his ſickle,
Hippocrates Magnus and Schuppachs Michel,
Galenus and Doctor Menadie,
With the Salernian Academy;

23. Not one of them found time for fleein',
Not Noftradamus nor fuperintendent Ziehen:
With doctor Fauft, dreamer Swedenburg, too,
He made a clean fweep and went through.

24. Orpheus, the great mufician,
Molière, the comedian of the Parifian nation,
And the famous painter Apellés,
Friend Death has fwept away all thefe.

25. The long-eared Midas, (all children know it,)
Homerus, the old blind beggar-poet,
Veftris the dancer and brave Tamerlane,
Struggled with the deftroyer in vain.

26. Ah yes, dear reader! with terrible grip he
Seized and devoured Penelope, Xanthippe,
Judith, Dido, Lucretia,
And the queen from far Arabia.

27. Cynic Timon, Democritus the laughing phyfician,
Juggler Schröpfer and Simon the magician,
Socrates and young Werther, the one
A wife man, t'other a fimpleton.

28. Bucephalus and Roffinante
And Abulabas the Elephant, he,
With the horfe Bayard and Balaam's afs,
Took for a morning meal like grafs.

29. Summa Summarum, the long and the fhort is,
That in none of the chronicles do we find notice,
That friend Death has ever any one paffed
Without coming back for him at laft.

30. And what he has not eaten already
He will not fail to remember when he's ready:
Alas! dear reader, alſo thee,
And, what is worſt of all, even me!

31. From the common lot (we've now to mention,)
Hieronimus, the watchman, found no exemption,
Him, too, friend Death removed from the ſtage,
When forty years and three weeks of age.

32. He caught an inflammatory fever
From which he might have recovered, however,
If they had only let natûre
That beſt of nurſes, work his cure.

33. But a doctor who in curing was mighty,
With a powerful doſe of Elixir Vitæ,
In the very beſt method carried him faſt
To the place where we all muſt go at laſt.

34. And now when to the grave they bore him,
The Schildeburgers did loudly deplore him,
For there had not, in many a century,
Been known ſuch a famous night watchman as he.

NOTE.

One is reminded by this chapter of "Father Mulvaney's Sarmon" in Mrs. Hall's Lights and Shadows of Iriſh Life: "Now you ſee that the great min of *ould* times are all dead! not a mortial ſowl of them all alive." . . . . . .

"There was Julus Caſar and twelve of them there was—*mortus est*—he's dead!" . . . . .

"There was the great Cleopatra, an Egyptian, and a great warrior; he uſed to drink *purls* for *wather—mortus est!* he's dead too! There was Marc Anthony, a grate frind and coajuthor of Cleopatra's, he had a grate turn for boating and the like—*mortus est*—he's dead too! There was Charley-mange, a grate Frinch man of larning and tongues, and with all his larning—*mortus est*—he's dead too! There was the grate Alexandre the gineral of the whole wide world—*mortus est*—he's dead too! . . . There was the grate Cicero, a mighty fine pracher like myself—*mortus est*—he's dead too!"

FIN—

CPSIA information can be obtained
at www.ICGtesting.com
Printed in the USA
LVHW101149040522
717864LV00003B/123